RÍO LOA
Station of Dreams

RÍO LOA
Station of Dreams

A NOVEL

LUDWIG ZELLER

Translated from Spanish by
A.F. Moritz & Theresa Moritz

Mosaic Press
TORONTO PARIS NEW YORK

Canadian Cataloguing in Publication Data

Zeller, Ludwig, 1927-
 [Rio Loa, estacion de los suenos. English]
 Rio Loa, station of dreams

Translation of: Rio Loa, estacion de los suenos.
ISBN 0-88962-658-8

I. Moritz, A.F. II. Moritz, Theresa. III. Title. IV. Title: Rio Loa, estacion de los
suenos. English.

PS8599.E45R5613 1999	C863	C99-930129-2
PR9199.3.Z44R5613 1999		

Published by MOSAIC PRESS, P.O. Box 1032, Oakville, Ontario, L6J 5E9,
Canada. Offices and warehouse at 1252 Speers Road, Units #1&2, Oakville,
Ontario, L6L 5N9, Canada and Mosaic Press, 85 River Rock Drive, Suite 202,
Buffalo, N.Y., 14207, USA.

Mosaic Press acknowledges the assistance of the Canada Council, the Ontario
Arts Council and the Dept. of Canadian Heritage, Government of Canada, for
their support of our publishing programme.

THE CANADA COUNCIL | LE CONSEIL DES ARTS
FOR THE ARTS | DU CANADA
SINCE 1957 | DEPUIS 1957

Printed and bound in Canada

MOSAIC PRESS, in Canada:
1252 Speers Road, Units #1&2, Oakville, Ontario, L6L 5N9
Phone / Fax: (905) 825-2130
E-mail: cp507@freenet.toronto.on.ca

MOSAIC PRESS, in the USA:
85 River Rock Drive, Suite 202, Buffalo, N.Y., 14207
Phone / Fax: 1-800-387-8992
E-mail: cp507@freenet.toronto.on.ca

TABLE OF CONTENTS

Toward the South 1

Station of Dreams 17

The Inconveniences of Virtue 25

The Ivory Moon 33

Shadows on the Sand 41

Two Cards and a Miracle 51

Living Dolls 61

Dinner with the Maestro 71

Sofía the Medium 77

The Strange History of Helena Ferrucchi 83

A Singular Day 91

Stringing Dreams Together 101

Double Wedding with Disguises 113

A Stormy Burial 123

The Tarot Cards 129

The Dance — Preparations and Dreams 137

The Dance — Images and the Wind 149

The Return 159

A NOTE ABOUT THE TRANSLATORS

A.F. MORITZ AND THERESA MORITZ have co-translated previous works from Spanish, including Gilberto Meza's *Testament for Man: Selected Poems* (1982) and Ludwig Zeller's collection of poems *Body of Insomnia* (1996). They have frequently travelled to Mexico and have published translations of several younger Mexican poets in journals. A.F. Moritz has translated three other books of Zeller's poetry published by Mosaic Press: *In The Country of Antipodes* (1979), *The Marble Head and Other Poems* (1986), and *The Ghost's Tattoos* (1989). He has also published translations from modern French poetry, notably *Children of the Quadrilateral: Selected Poems of Benjamin Péret* (1978).

The Moritzes met Ludwig Zeller and his wife Susana Wald in 1978 and have worked with them, on occasion, ever since. In 1994, Zeller and A.F. Moritz published *Phantoms in the Ark*, a collage-poem in which a long poem by Moritz was coordinated with a sequence of 36 collages by Zeller. Widely known for his own poetry, A.F. Moritz is a lecturer in creative writing at Victoria College. Theresa Moritz, who teaches English literature at the University of Toronto, is the co-author with Judson Allen of *A Distinction of Stories: The Medieval Unity of Chaucer's Canterbury Tales*, (1981). In addition to the doctorate in medieval studies Moritz holds a master's degree in Spanish literature. The Moritzes have co-written such nonficiton books as *Stephen Leacock: A Biography* (1985), *The Oxford Literary Guide to Canada* (1987), and the forthcoming *Emma Goldman in Canada*.

To my parents, to Ida, on the other side of the invisible wall.

To my brothers and sisters who lived or were born, as I was, in Río Loa, to all those who some time or other have heard me speak of that mythic place.

He who dreams that he is dreaming
is about to awake.

— Novalis

Because there is nothing in this world
more interesting than humanity.
And in humanity, most interesting
is the interior life.
And in the interior life, most mysterious
are those profound depths
revealed to us in dreams.

— Evelyne Weileumann

Toward the South

Packing always aggravates me. It interrupts my work, and I have to forecast the days ahead: in a way, to pack is to challenge fate. What clothes I should wear, what documents I'll need, what books should be with me for that moment when I arrive at my hotel—always strange, inhospitable—and that later moment of summoning sleep that doesn't come, reading the same page over and over.

But it's Susana who packs my bag, making all the necessaries fit as into a Chinese box. What's more, she'll draw up a list of all my things so I won't forget any on returning.

A month ago I received an invitation to participate in a writers' congress in Sante Fe, "Surrealism in the New World." Envelope and letter bore the address of the Alliance Française; a man I supposed was the director was asking me to read from my work, but the note was handwritten and the signature illegible. It sat on my table for a couple of weeks until, one day, the mailman brought me a new letter repeating the request. It seemed almost an obligation. I'd have to go.

The weather was hot. For the first time in several weeks it felt as if summer had returned. I read the note over: yes, it would seem I had to depart for the south, consort with some old friends, exchange books, see women pass before my eyes like burning coals.

So there I was, between anxiety and distraction, watching my wife fill my suitcases, including medicines, sleeping pills, and an old Bible I always consult before falling asleep. Let's see, then: what would it say? It opened to St. John, chapter 13, verse 2. I read: "And during the supper, the devil having already put it into the heart of Judas Iscariot, the son of Simon, to betray him, Jesus, knowing that the Father had given all things into his hands, and that he had come forth from God and was going to God, rose from the supper and laid aside his garments, and taking a towel girded himself."

An odd note to start a journey on, I said to myself. I kissed the page in accord with the ritual custom, closed the book and put it among my shirts. It was getting late: time had passed almost without my noticing. Where was my ticket? In my briefcase—of course. I get nervous; it's clear I'm no good at this.

The car's not working, Susana told me with an expression between serious and amused. It'll be a good idea if we call a taxi. Airplanes and trains wait for no man, you have to take care of yourself, keep alert for small details. You can't be so absent-minded.

We barged down the front steps, hastily saying good-bye. My bags were out front and it appeared that the cab had already arrived. A thin, gaunt man made a gesture something like a greeting and fit the luggage into the trunk. His strength surprised me—he was very short and skinny yet handled the suitcases as if they were feathers. I settled myself on a back seat that seemed excessively large and plush, and sank into it so far that I could hardly see the driver's rather sparse hair. I sighed deeply. At last the journey was beginning. I had no idea how time was passing or what avenues we crossed, for the windows were darkly tinted and it was impossible to make out details of the streets. How long did the ride take? I don't remember. Sometimes I think it was years.

The taxi stopped, the door opened, the driver's small head appeared, strangely resembling that of a ram. The man's solemn manner was accentuated by the threadbare black uniform he wore. Attentively he helped me climb out. Yes! We were at Union Station, full of people trying to force their way through the crowd and the stacks of luggage, or saying their good-byes, or meeting friends after many years. Everyone was shouting at the same time, greeting or insulting one another in foreign tongues: true cacophony.

My driver meanwhile opened a path among the suitcases, baskets and bundles. I couldn't help noticing his almost animal ability to avoid obstacles, to get around them. We soon reached our train, whose cars were strangely empty: one woman in black next to a window and one man dressed with a rather extravagant old-fashioned elegance were the only other occupants of my coach.

Everything was in order: now I could settle my thoughts and prepare for what I would have to do in the coming days.

We were on our way!

I heard a whistle and the train slowly began to move, like a snake dragging itself through the night. For a while I tried to sleep but without success. Had much time passed?

The car was dimly lit and the darkness outside made it seem we were advancing through a black tunnel. I got up and went to the lavatory: maybe wetting my head would dissipate the drowsiness that had overcome me. It was a good thought, for the cold water woke me up. Where was I?

The train went on, creaking and grating through the night.

I walked back down the long, empty car and stopped by the seat of the woman dressed in austere black. She was almost motionless. It seemed she was looking at something far off, beyond the windows, which I could not see, out where the gusty fog was thickening.

To my good evening she responded with a good evening like an echo coming from some distant elsewhere. Slowly she turned toward me and with a reluctant gesture of her hand seemed to invite me to sit down. Pardon me, I said, making myself comfortable in the seat across from her. I hope I'm not bothering you but today's the first night of our long trip south and I thought maybe you wouldn't mind chatting—it's stiflingly hot in here and there's probably no hope of sleep.

She smiled, or I thought I could detect a smile, though a veil networked with small "moon" dots covered her face and a ribboned hat coquettishly shaded its mystery.

I lit a cigarette. Maybe she'll want to smoke, I said to myself, and that way I'll see her. But she made a negative gesture, as though divining my thought. "Fire of any sort always makes me remember the other fire." Her voice was remote and thin, as though she were trying not to attract attention. However, she continued, to each his own.

I agreed with a grin. Doubtless this woman was in mourning or something of the sort; her impeccably tailored suit and the fur coat on the coat hook made it clear she was a wealthy lady, very reserved out of some private motive but extraordinarily attractive nonetheless. Not having much idea of how to get a conversation going, I too turned my face to the thick window panes and tried to pick out something in the darkness.

After a while, when my eyes had adjusted, I saw that the swarms and masses in the outer shadow were trees, or maybe rock formations, which resembled strange black-on-black buildings.

The woman was looking right toward me now, as if through or behind me some other landscape was unwinding. Who was she? Did she have a name? Tension increased in me, keeping pace with a growing sense of stupid and somewhat lewd torpor.

I felt an irresistible, almost animal desire to be with this woman, to lean my head on her shoulder.

I don't know if it was I who spoke and asked her her name.

I heard an echo like a distant laugh, and a sound, now nearby:

Helena. Yes, an old-fashioned name, one my parents liked.

I felt that a wall between us had been breached. But it was nonsensical to tell her I was overjoyed. It's as if, sometimes, beings don't seem to exist until we know their names, I told her. Yours is a beautiful name—full of mythological resonances. She seemed not to hear my words.

Helena! Mysterious Helena, embarked on that long journey to the distant south. My knees seemed to stretch out on their own account to touch hers. If only for a single moment she would let me glimpse her face! Curiosity made me fumble my words and fall into long silences. A perfume of burnt herbs and grasses now overcame me: it was a fragrance of autumn fields, a sweetness of drying flowers scattered in the wind. From time to time I noticed the noise of the train advancing into blackness, gliding like a stream of radiance through the night. Could I possibly ask her to show me her face?

I got up my courage like someone preparing to cross a powerful river. Helena, I said, and I could hear my voice trembling. You're an enchanting person, but I think some sorrow is hurting you. Tell me: can't I help you? Sometimes sorrow wraps us in its veil, but maybe... My sentence hung in the air.

Ludwig, neither you nor anyone can help me. Her voice was melancholy, and as slow as if she were counting the syllables. You act exactly the way you did when you were a child. You're still trying to trick me.

Her tone had become familiar now as she scolded me for something I failed to understand. How could it be that she'd seen me when I was a small boy, especially since she wasn't nearly my age?

I reached out my hand and lightly touched her leg and said, Maybe there's a game of lies and a game of truths and they're the same game. If I'm acting like a child, it's only because you don't want to show me your face.

We were directly opposite and she, after hesitating for a moment, said, Well then, look at me.

I reached over and opened her veil, full of desire to drink in her visage. But there was no face there, the most beautiful of all faces I was expecting was not there. And in the space that corresponded to the neck there opened a turbulent pit, deep in which life was writhing. But there was no head.

Horror and fascination left me motionless.

Don't you want to gaze at me, don't you intend to console me now? hissed a voice that came from the depths—from that hollow that was her throat—like an echo, like an invocation. I watched absorbed as a thick, white, textured substance slowly rose from the neck. A cauli-flower! So it was. A cauliflower that was speaking words to me as though from the nakedness of a face. No melancholy eyes, no tremulous lips. A cauliflower. Beyond all imagining.

I felt that everything was freezing around me, that I had no true notion of what was happening.

Helena! Helena! It was simply the train penetrating the fissures of the night. The train had torn the night's veil.

When my eyes opened again I heard someone, supporting my head, say, Drink! Drink this water. Another hand was moistening my forehead.

I found myself stretched out on one of the train seats and the gentleman I'd noticed as possessing a somewhat bizarre elegance was trying to revive me and was smiling.

It's nothing serious. Sometimes the heat can make you faint. Or maybe you slipped in the aisle? I didn't know how to answer: there beside him stood the mysterious woman in black, smiling from a lovely face that made me forget everything that had happened before as if it had been only a nightmare.

The conductor brought me a whiskey with ice. Drink this, distin-guished sir, he said with that ingratiating amiability displayed by cer-tain servants who've had the opportunity to see many things in this world. His face reminded me of the taxi driver's. In fact, there could be no doubt—it was the same person: perhaps an additional service on this southbound express.

When I felt restored, the gentleman—whom I'd taken for a sales-man—presented himself courteously. Allow me to introduce myself: Leonardo, or simply, the Maestro, as my friends like to call me. And this, he continued, is the Contessa Helena Ferrucchi, who is traveling with us across the earth to forget her grief. I nodded, looking from one of them to the other. The conductor too made me a respectful bow and said: Asmodeus, the Old One, at your service.

I did not know very well how to repay the consideration my traveling companions were showing me; I wanted to say something equally gracious, but I felt suffocated.

The Maestro took the initiative: Rest, dear friend, we're going to have plenty of time to talk and exchange our thoughts. The trip's a long one and you seem exhausted. It will be better if you sleep. I looked at the woman in black, the Contessa Helena Ferrucchi, and saw she was smiling. How clear and distinct her face appeared to me at that instant! Maybe Maestro Leonardo was right: best to close my eyes and sleep.

By the time I woke it was broad daylight. Every trace of discomfort had disappeared with the shadows. The Maestro had ordered places for four to be set in the dining car, and it was with pleasure that after washing my face I joined my fellow travelers at a table covered with fruits and exotic foods.

I wanted you, said Helena Ferrucchi, to try these rare delicacies from the south, and these fruits that wither anywhere but under the tropic sun.

Light streamed in from all the windows now and outside we saw an unfolding landscape of cactus and enormous varicolored rocks. Is this the Mojave Desert, I wondered. As if he knew what I was thinking, Asmodeus—dressed now in an impeccable black and white uniform— pointed to a sign at the edge of the roadbed: "Labyrinth of Memory." I laughed to see it and said to my companions: If the name really matches the place, maybe we're going to meet some entertainment.

The Maestro and the Contessa talked about images as they picked at fruits coated in sugar. I was looking at the man's mysterious aquiline profile when he turned to me and said: You will meet, my dear poet, greater realities than you've yet imagined. I know you had your doubts about taking this trip. Now the important thing is, precisely, to ask for— to demand—the impossible.

This made me smile to myself. Wasn't I always seeking the impossible? So, I exclaimed, here we are, flying south like so many birds, and you have to remind me of my everyday troubles. They all laughed.

Asmodeus uncorked a bottle labeled Cactus Flower and we decided to drink to the success of our enterprise. Helena Ferrucchi suggested that we should all form the "cube of good luck," a toast in which everyone drinks from another's glass. It's infallible, she said. We'll all achieve our most secret desires. Rapidly the liquor disappeared from the glasses and we each grew certain that our most violent hopes were going to be satisfied.

The Maestro, seated to my left, drew nearer to me as though to tell a secret. His hands held a deck of cards that looked like an old-fashioned Tarot; riffling it with his fingers, he quoted: "Sometimes wolves sing like nightingales," and went on, "I see here that Fortune's Wheel is turning, that every desire will be fulfilled, and it will happen while this moon is still in the sky. We're going to see what was invisible." He laughed and gave me a friendly pat on the shoulder. This moved me to try to treat him more familiarly in return. How well you speak Spanish, I said, where did you learn it? I saw a spark of pride in his eyes. I'm a polyglot, he answered. Only when I speak the dead languages do I have any trace of my local accent, but since I rarely use them, most of my friends just assume that my native tongue is German.

I caught a melancholy trace in his eyes. Alas, I told him, it's a language I heard in my childhood, but it's become to me like one of those old tunes that haunts us all our days and we can never remember the words.

He smiled sadly. The landscape in the windows flew by, our speed making immense rocky plains and trees and houses suddenly appear and disappear.

Helena Ferrucchi asked me jibingly, What would be the first wish of a poet who's rising on the Wheel of Fortune? Her eyes flickered as though she were trading guesses with the Maestro. I didn't know what to say to her. Would anyone but me be able to grasp those days of my childhood that sometimes return in my dreams? I'm not exactly sure, I answered, and besides, the memory of happy times always drags us back down into sorrow.

For that one moment I felt we all shared the same belief.

Then the Maestro stirred himself: Enough gloom! Whatever the poet wants most deeply, he shall have. I noticed his fingers shuffling and manipulating the worn cards as if to distract him from deeper worries.

Slowly now we filed back to our seats in our own car.

The Maestro wore a faded black suit, and over his shoulders hung a cloak whose fur collar shone with reddish glints. He leaned on a walking stick with a gold handle, but I believe it was mainly an old-style affectation, maybe one of those ancient Venetian stilettos encased in an elegant cylinder of bamboo. I offered my arm to the beautiful Helena. With the rocking of the train I could feel how slender she was, as though I were moving some delicate structure covered in silks. Her arm, crossed on mine, was cold; as I looked intently at her long fingers, she smiled and said: My fingertips have been worn away by love-making, but a different fire cools my body. I laughed a bit, like someone receiving a confidence. Asmodeus, who'd prepared a veritable fountain of unusual liquors and a feast of tidbits, followed us humming some old song.

Helena went back to her own seat. As though casually, she told me: I've loved without rest, besieged by the desire of thousands of men. And it's always the same. But now it seems that after years I've found something different.

The Maestro interrupted to invite me to have a look at some old books and I sat down in the seat across from his. We opened the long folding table between us and, like all experienced gamblers, rubbed our hands briskly before beginning to examine the books. A little dram of curiosity before perusing the invisible, my companion whispered. Asmodeus, bring the poet a glass of passion fruit and ice. The servingman ran to bring us a drink as red as blood. He left the bottle and we settled back in the thickly padded seats, I facing north and the Maestro opposite me, looking in the train's direction as it galloped neighing southward. I noticed again the Maestro's worn pack of cards with their engravings discolored by long use.

Now you're traveling backward, he said, referring to my position. Believe me, your wishes are sure to come true. Then he opened out a sort of scroll similar to certain Japanese paintings and revealed a living map of the places we were traveling through, entirely covered with a substance that seemed like crystal floating on the landscape. The train goes along this way, he said, it makes a more pleasant trip for you, and it will give us time to talk over our old passions. He rapped on that pane-like substance on the map scroll and as if we had suddenly come much nearer to it, or as if we were looking at the world it depicted through an immense magnifying glass, we saw the dry plains of northern Mexico slowly opening out around us. I know there are places you miss, he said carefully, but maybe it would be better if you don't stop at Stone River, since that might mean some sort of fall or disaster. I agreed, surprised that he knew about my weakness for the home town of a pair of sisters I had loved unrequited. I didn't know what to say and looked distractedly out the window, where the landscapes I had seen on the scroll passed one by one.

Smiling then and looking into the Maestro's face, I said: I'd like to page through some books that I only know from my dreams. There are certain minute volumes that I come across in my dream wanderings: I carefully stow them in my pockets but when I wake up they're not there. Once a good friend of mine from Venice showed me an edition of Dante, but I only remember the gilt covers, not the insides.

My companion looked partly amused, partly annoyed. There are small errors in your memory, he said. The book you saw was Petrarch's *Rime* published by F. Ongania more than a century ago. If you want to see scenes from the *Commedia* I'll show you Boss's edition, put out by the Amsterdam alchemists a couple of centuries earlier. He took from his pocket a small book with a black cover bearing oriental characters; inside, the text was mixed with extremely vivid, even living, pictures that moved across the pages from edge to edge and seemed to want to speak to me.

I was like someone staring into a mirage. Up mountains in high relief climbed men dragging heavy smoking stones: the whole scene was alive. What the figures were reciting were tercets by the great Florentine poet, what we were looking at was his Hell itself. I was transfixed, ecstatic, watching the old images that had gained a new life.

These are illusions, masquerades, said the Maestro emphatically. Dark illusions of an exile. Sometimes I used to think that in him I'd found a friend, but we all make mistakes.

I saw again that air of sadness in my fellow traveler. You yourself know, you must remember, he said, fixing his eyes on my face. I asked you years ago to write a history of my life, I was going to help you gather the materials for the text and for the collages you would have made to illustrate it.

I tried to recall. True, in a dream the devil once had appeared to me and handed over a thick leather-bound tome; its pages were blank and I was supposed to write on them what he would dictate in the form of memories. I remembered the dream distinctly. But did this mean that the Maestro, this bibliophile who was obviously a master illusionist, was the devil? My thoughts turned somersaults and I had no idea what to do.

The Maestro was smiling across the table. Childhood terrors, dear poet. Illusions that become reality. Yes, my name's Leonardo...one of my many modern names. Indeed it was I who gave you a blank book where you could take down from dictation all things that occur. But it looks, my friend, as if you were too afraid: and I'm only a sad reflection of what each person carries inside—the inner demon.

I rearranged myself in the seat and looked closely at the Maestro, talking there in front of me as though from behind a pane of glass: a man seemingly in his fifties, elegant in his gray-black suit. His hairy hands showed long nails and a pair of glittering rings. But it was his face above all that claimed my attention. One might have said it was made of dry, singed wood, and in his eyes great liveliness alternated with a fixed melancholy, as if he were completely skeptical that anyone could ever love him.

Then all at once I remembered a dream.

A question had been proposed to me: did I want to go up or down. I decided to go up and I saw myself climbing stone steps behind a person who seemed enveloped in a cape that fluttered in the wind. I couldn't see his face.

Only when we had reached the upper part of an immense cupola and were looking down on a seacoast covered with palm trees did I turn toward him and recognize he was the devil, sad, sunk in a profound depression. He said not a word; like me, he was watching a twilight sketched with red clouds in a stormy sky fall across that coast. I realized then that he was keeping silent due to the revulsion and fear his face aroused in me. And so he continued not to speak to me, not to offer a single word.

Next I saw smoke come from his mouth, move downward, thicken, and slowly take what seemed to be a human form: it became a beautiful woman who was crying—crying over my rejection of the devil's face. I tried to explain that it was an irrational reaction, that I knew we will all lose our bodily forms and become dust, that the matter wrapping our bones is as much an illusion as our fear of the devil, the streaked and furrowed mirror we all carry within. But I did not really understand what relationship there could be between that beautiful girl who had appeared in the smoke and the face that so horrified me.

Nevertheless I promised her to try to understand, to talk with this being who was terrifying and tormented at the same time. She stopped crying and the smoke dissipated, as if he who had emitted it had now swallowed it again. Then I suggested to the devil that we descend the steps to the beach. We did so, fairly running downward. And upon arriving at the beach I found that the person running in front of me was my friend Mario Espinosa, a handsome-looking red-haired man, who turned around to me, laughing aloud. Could he be the devil?

Illusions, illusions! I said to myself. Every time we bring an image from our personal myths down to the human level, it takes on the human condition and its weaknesses.

The ocean out there before me kept on milling the centuries.

The Maestro was watching me from across the table.

A long silence ensued, and finally I heard him, as though talking to himself, begin to murmur regretful phrases on the subject of his desire to understand humans and be loved by them. Then, seeming to put sad thoughts behind him, he started to discuss books again. Here's one with marble covers, of Japanese origin I suppose, or maybe Hindu, that hides a whole series of secrets about love. He thought for a moment, and then: Small errors are always accumulating in one's memory. There are ruined temples, virtually complete monuments with passages and galleries where all the forms of passion play out: some call them "The Stones of Ecstasy." Much of all this has been destroyed because what people fear most is their own lust and the way it drags them along. Still, there were a few who preserved those temples in sketches and petitioned me for new forms of the madness of love, of possessing what one truly loves. They created tiny books that can be hidden, they covered them with jewels, they perfumed them, they bound them in painted marble carvings. There's no doubt about it, it's certain of these books, translated from stone to paper, that you've seen.

I nodded. My companion was describing the same little books I had dreamed. I saw that he was groping through pockets in his cape and suddenly from its folds emerged a bird like a pheasant, with a woman's head. She walked slowly along the table and put her face close to mine, and I could see and hear and feel her tears falling. I was shocked into speechlessness, and now I noticed too that instead of the legs of a bird this being had diminutive female calves and thighs.

I sensed the Maestro examining me from his side of the table.

Ludwig Zeller, he said, can it be that you don't remember what you yourself have written? I wasn't able to recover from my astonishment: this face, watching me from the shore of tears.

Well, he said finally, I see that time's getting short. I make you a gift of this bird which, whenever you like, will be either the book with marble covers or the woman you dream is living in its pages. Leonardo petted the pheasant's head and it changed immediately into a little book, which he handed to me across our table. Remember, it's both a book and an amulet by which you can always summon the woman-bird.

Taking the little volume I looked in his eyes and said, Thanks: for the second time you're giving me a book. In the first one I could have written and drawn your story. And now in this one I have a magic bird that can change itself into a woman and teach me all the knots of love. But what can I give you?

The Maestro thought for an instant and said: You've looked at my face and into my eyes with trust. Now you're traveling back to a place where beloved people and things are going to appear very strange to you. Maybe you'd allow us to come along. The noise of bankers counting money bores me, I prefer the company of poets—for them illusions are daily bread. I gave him my hand to make it a deal.

The train was running now between low hills and the arid landscape seemed somehow familiar. It was four or five in the afternoon and the moon had just begun to rise above the horizon.

As I looked out, an unprecedented feeling of plenitude overcame me. I thought of the book, of my bizarre traveling companions, the bird with a woman's face. Where were we headed for? The Maestro put his arm around my shoulder and pointed out, in the distance, a train station standing in the middle of the desert. It was oddly familiar, and as the train approached it my half-conscious suspicion became a certainty.

We passed several train cars and finally came to a sign announcing the name of the place: Río Loa.

Here we are, said the Maestro, the station of dreams.

A large crowd was excitedly milling about outside. Brakes screeched, halting the train in which we had made such a long journey. Bright multicolored costumes filled the platform: *chola* women selling the widest imaginable assortment of goods—stones, fruits, flowers. There were my parents, waving to me, showing they'd expected my arrival. The Maestro got out first, then Helena Ferrucchi, followed by me, shaken by the power of my emotions, and finally Asmodeus, who had taken charge of all the luggage that was with us: boxes and more boxes filled with I had no idea what.

Station of Dreams

 had to open a way for myself through the villagers crowding the station. Each one wanted to embrace me, say something personal. Finally I reached and hugged my parents, overjoyed to see them. For an instant the thought crossed my mind, "But they're dead," at which my father laughed, "But son, that was another reality." It seemed that a true welcome-home party had been organized. Behind me, the Maestro was observing my reactions. I started to present him to my father but they greeted each other as old friends. German phrases fluttered in my ears. The Maestro, it emerged, had met him in India at the beginning of the century, and they laughed and joked about old times. Courteously, the Maestro greeted my mother and presented Helena Ferrucchi and Asmodeus the Old One, who was busily running hither and yon packing our possessions into a sort of bus. In the crowd all around us I recognized childhood friends, neighbors and various persons apparently in charge of the reception.

My beautiful teacher, Zoila Campana, covered with veils and wearing a hat the wind threatened to carry off at every moment, came forward solemnly, curtsied, and said to all four of us new arrivals: I give you greetings from Río Loa the Eternal, who welcomes you as her children. Her words were lost in applause and the voices of children singing an old song: "....When you go away, shadows will wrap all around me." Zoila was upset: it seemed the children had made a mistake and were not singing the song that had been chosen to give a specially joyful

13

brilliance to my welcome.

Then Father decided we should leave so that we could be properly received at home. Asmodeus preceded us in the bus full of children and boxes. Awaiting us were two elegant green limousines, enormous, with the severe air of hearses. The station master waved affectionately in my direction; Don Ricardo Lorca hadn't changed, his cap with its little metal badge seemed to make him taller than the average man. He was worried about the huge commotion at his station and we decided to set out immediately in the ancient cars.

As we drove along, my father and the Maestro recalling old adventures, we passed the dynamite factory and Helena asked my mother if there were many accidents. They're rare, Mother said, and they seem to coincide with other, parallel events happening in people's inner lives.

The afternoon had brought me shocks and joys I had only dreamed of. What now seemed like a dream was the convention in Santa Fe I was supposedly attending. And I gathered that the train we had taken in fact only ever arrives at Río Loa, or maybe sometimes at Calama; the locomotive and cars had been left sitting at the railway crossing in the station yard, and this didn't seem to worry anyone, at least for the time being. We were all plunged in childish happiness as our automobiles rolled slowly, ceremoniously toward the village two kilometers away.

From far off I could see that the whole place was glowing with light. We stopped in front of my parents' house and my brother and sisters ran out to greet us, hugging us and joking. Everything seemed newly cleaned, the wind wasn't blowing, and trees in flower surrounded all the houses. I didn't know what to think, everything seemed radiant, everybody I met was happy, exalted, as if he or she had just had a very strong, very stimulating drink.

My brother Carlos told me that a few minutes earlier an enormous bus had arrived, filled with the school children accompanied by a pleasant man who had snapped his fingers and, like a magician, made an enormous profusion of plants sprout up and flower. With an aspergill from one of his boxes he had run around and sprinkled the entire village, which now was very brightly decked out, as if for a party. All of this in the blink of an eye.

We still have to find out, my brother said, if the lady with you and this magician who's put so much color into the village will accept lodgings at the guest hostel. You'll stay with us, at home, and the Maestro—he seems like a distinguished man—Doctor and Señora Sarabia have offered to put him up. You know, they're very good people and they'll treat him with the utmost deference. My parents and I agreed to all this and it turned out that Asmodeus had already talked with the Sarabias and taken a room with them for the Maestro.

To everyone's delight, Carlos related how Asmodeus, since we had no rugs at home, had opened some of the boxes and brought out beautiful Persian carpets, as well as crystal ware and bottles containing what looked to be the costliest liquors. Everything seemed done by magic. They had all wanted, it was true, to receive me with a great show of affection, but now happiness was bordering on complete madness.

Asmodeus had performed like the magician he was and won the admiration of all who met him. And with her languid beauty, Helena had cast into a waking dream every man lucky enough to see her. Río Loa was suffering an attack of joy. I was from the village and its feeling for me was natural, but the presence of my companions was beyond anyone's expectation. Above all they couldn't stop thinking about the distinguished gentleman in the dark shining suit and the hat with a red feather.

My father accompanied the guests to their rooms so they could arrange their belongings and invited them all to a small dinner the village was throwing two hours later in the place's one social club.

Meanwhile I walked through all of the few streets gazing at one house after the other, and the small village square, the school, the general store, and a few other buildings that I didn't remember or that had been built since my time. I discovered that the people hadn't changed: was the contentment that I was feeling shaping my impression of the place? Evening was falling and the hills took on iridescent colors; shadows were blue and the air quiet. In the distance the first lights came on in Calama, and still farther off Chuquicamata too could now be seen.

The club was an enclosed place seating about 300 people, and I noticed that improvements made since I'd last seen the establishment fit in perfectly with the sprucing up that Asmodeus' hyssop had accomplished. When it was completely dark, Father went in search of our visitors and found them rambling — just as I had done a few hours before— through the little village and exclaiming over it in delight.

On entering the hall the Maestro noticed the large table that had been brought from the kitchen of our house. Smiling, he said to Mother that everything appropriate had been done, but that he too wanted to help host this meal, at which the whole village had come together to help in our reception. With an elegant gesture, our guest let his cape drop on the back of his chair and, his fingers crossed, signaled to Asmodeus, who seemed to have been waiting for this gesture. At once Asmodeus left and returned burdened down with several large trays from which all the tables were quickly filled with delicacies.

The happiness I had noticed in the village ever since arriving had actually increased. The finest liquors were being served in tall glasses of Bohemian crystal and this quickly made all the people at the tables much more talkative. The bottles seemed to refill themselves automatically, and even the most timid people grew exultant, and told things that for years they had kept hidden in their hearts.

Our table too was served the same rare foods and liquors and everyone accepted them as the most natural thing in the world. Next to us Doctor Sarabia laughed, proud that his hospitality had been accepted, and his wife Inés, a brunette of about thirty, beamed resplendently. As always she wore a veil, but on this evening it was transparent as air and glittering with diminutive lights.

Everyone kept telling me all at once that they'd been waiting for my visit for years, that they couldn't be happier; they were grateful, too, that such distinguished friends had accompanied me. Each one wanted to hear news of my travels and was eager to know if I had with me such and such a book to show them. Truly this last question took me off guard: it hadn't occurred to me to bring along the modest editions brought out for me by friends and publishers in Canada. The Maestro said then: Since I'm a book collector, there'll certainly be some examples in the boxes Asmodeus has brought along. At once Asmodeus produced a number of my titles and put them out on the tables, where they were objects of curiosity to friends who had known me since childhood.

Between talk and toasts midnight was approaching and Father suggested that we mustn't tire such worthy visitors; he thanked them for their presence in Río Loa and regretted the lack of an adequate ballroom, where he might have invited everyone to end such an extraordinary evening with dancing. The Maestro, who endured all this rhetoric somewhat absent-mindedly, whispered in my father's ear that in the next few days he would see about finding a place for such a party, which would allow him to repay all the attentions he had received that evening. Amid songs and music that seemed to reverberate in the walls, we left the hall; Father again accompanied each of the visitors to their lodgings, while my brother and sisters and I amused them with lively stories and recollections of local legends. As arranged, Asmodeus and the beautiful Helena remained in the village's guest hostel. As we said our farewells she winked at me and said: We'll meet each other in dreams. Good night.

The Maestro was put up in the Sarabias' small house, opposite ours, and I went by to ask if he wanted anything. Laughing, he grasped my shoulders and said: Everyone's wishes will be satisfied. We'll talk tomorrow about organizing some trips into the countryside. I noted that Leonardo's room was dim and that he had arranged to have candles lit. Old habit, he said. Now get some rest—in the next few days we'll have a lot of work to do and our hearts will be full of feeling. We embraced and I went home. Now I was able to take a leisurely look at the old pepper trees I had climbed in my childhood and whose every branch I knew intimately, whose flowers exhaled a penetrating fragrance all around the house, as the branches entwined on the beams of the porch. My mother had prepared my bed and with her usual loving care had omitted not a single detail. I kissed her and my sisters and decided— I felt that my body could scarcely support me a moment longer—to go to sleep. I was here, the wanderer returned, looking at the boards of my old bedroom's ceiling. Within an instant a dream had enveloped me: I heard a rooster crowing nearby, probably next door at the house of Zoila Campana, my teacher. Maybe that poor animal of hers was still alive, or maybe they had bought another one.

The wind began to rise and blow toward the pampas, a sound as soft as a lament. The moon was bending down over the horizon.

Slowly I fell into the dream, mirror of multiple prisms.

"I found myself in a populous city. I was walking on the righthand sidewalk of an immense poplar-lined boulevard with a park full of trees and potted flowers down its center. It was a customary walk for me, by which I went to my work at the Ministry of Education ten blocks ahead. The streets there have a slight incline, but this was more evident to me now than usual. Two blocks before I arrived, a painter friend of mine, Julio Aciares, approached. Anguished, he told me that I shouldn't go to the Ministry building: a grave accusation had been made against me, that I had stolen some paper. I laughed at first, the charge seemed to me so absurdly false, but my friend insisted, pulling at my arm so that I wouldn't continue walking. When he realized that, no matter what, I was going to go on, I saw him transformed into a photographer, a kindly

friend named Guevara. We had crossed the square in front of the Palacio de la Moneda, the presidential palace, and thus were at the corner of the block where the Ministry of Education stood. I clearly saw a pharmacy there and went into this building next door to my destination. The light grew each instant more peculiar, like the light during an eclipse. Guevara came with me to the elevator, which seemingly he operated, but he explained that it couldn't go up or down because a terrible accident had occurred. What was it?

I noticed then that the walls of the elevator didn't exist and that large splinters and shattered pieces of wood came up through cracks in the floor.

Indeed, it could neither rise nor descend. We were in a hospital and we saw with horror that the doors were being walled up. The accident had been something horrific that put all of us in danger. At first I tried to leave, but soon realized it was impossible; the wreckage and everything around us gave the place an infernal atmosphere, like a nightmare.

Then I took an immense hammer and other tools and started to break the windows, trying somehow to open a way out, and encountered iron bars. Guevara, skeptical, helped me almost out of inertia.

From other rooms, situated high up near the roof, we heard the voices of sick people or prisoners warning us to hurry our work, above all to break the windows and let in fresh air. Seemingly the illness or evil, whatever it might be, was fast at work and consisted of five small children: two little boys and three girls who were continuously transforming themselves. The two boys were like Fausts: one was false, evil, and the other good, but the false one could not be told apart from his companion except by the beard he wore on his childish face. The girls were a year or two older, but all seemed to suffer from some kind of skin condition. One of these girls, or fallen angels, caressed another, who repulsed her, saying she found love repugnant. I saw them at first behind the bars, later through a thick plastic film, and finally right beside me.

Did they have a contagious disease? Was that the evil? Was it a lack of love? I didn't know, it seemed to me that everyone was condemned to some horrible fate and that we would never find a way out, because every exit was walled off from the outside. We were besieged by plague, an evil we could not identify had befallen us. What could I do?"

The Inconveniences of Virtue

woke to the laughter of my brother and sisters eating breakfast in the next room. A quick shower washed away the effects of my dream, and I put on light clothes and joined them at table. The events of the day before had made me see that our joy was likely due in part to the fact that all of us were at an ideal age. Katty, my oldest sister, was the sixteen- or seventeen-year-old I remembered from childhood; blooming, sensuous, with a hunger for life. Carlos seemed to be the same sort of age, a young man around twenty, blond and extraordinarily agreeable in manner but at times touched by melancholy. Ida was running from place to place, making jokes, black wavy hair framing her smiling face. Very attractive, impassioned by every topic she talked about, she was part of the shouting that had woken me up. Kuni, my beloved Kuni, sparkled with golden braids down to her shoulders and looked on with curiosity at all the breakfast debating. Our meeting this way seemed natural to me. That I lived in Canada, that fifty years had passed, seemed an illusion which needn't concern me. Maybe it was only a dream.

Seeing my parents enter the dining room made me understand we were living a moment of magic. Mother: always so careful of her clothes, her dress so white, to the point of seeming transparent, in contrast with her jet black hair gathered into a beautiful knot from which it streamed down her back. She and my father looked at one another tenderly; he also was young and strong, full of that disposition of his that had power to move mountains.

19

We laughed and made plans. Most of all, we were simply delighting in finding ourselves reunited, and celebrating our visitors. It seemed the same euphoric state reigned in the whole village. Joking with one another, we went out to see some friends I wanted to talk to.

We opened doors and windows and the air carried in the fragrance of the flowers from the garden. From the porch we saw in the distance the silhouettes of volcanoes, snow-covered at the peaks, sending up plumes of smoke that dissipated in the air.

Then Doctor Sarabia came running from the other side of the street; rubbing his hands together, he walked up to our house. We greeted him and Mother offered him coffee. No, thank you, Señora Rosa, he told her, I've had a marvelous and a terrible night and it's only the pleasure and horror that make me run over to tell you what's happened.

We noticed his suit was rumpled and covered with dirt as if he had been rolling on the ground.

He hadn't put his glasses on, yet he looked happy to us, although with a touch of fear too in his expression.

It so happens, he began, that a little after you came by my house last night, I went out on the porch to look at the moon, which seemed enormous, and Villavicencio, Emiliano Rosso and Gaona were passing. We went to the square, which was deserted by that time, to talk over everything that had happened at dinner. We'd drunk a lot, maybe too much; anyway, we saw, passing along in front of the trees, a beautiful woman that none of us recognized. She walked by, very lightly dressed, and it seemed to us that as she went she made a beckoning gesture in our direction. All of us as a group immediately decided to go along with her: it was late at night and since maybe she didn't know the area, she might need something. We joined her and she went walking with an air of determination down the old Street of Skulls. Each of us felt as if she were inviting him in particular, she was so lovely and voluptuous, and as she walked the wind opened her skirt and showed us irresistible charms. We reached a stand of trees and she said she was tired and sat down on the grass. The four of us were so enthralled looking at her that we fell to our knees beside her. Her clothing and manner showed she was a woman of dignity and importance, but an irresistible desire seized us to lie next to her, to make love to her right there, on the grass. She laughed and joked with us—it was clear she could see right through us. She took off her velvet skirt, which changed color suddenly from black to fiery red, and we saw her flesh gleaming in the light of the moon like a delicious forbidden fruit.

20

Doctor Sarabia spoke so passionately of his night's adventures that there was no way to cut in on him. He was laughing and panting just from thinking about what had happened. With irrepressible lust we threw ourselves on her and I swear that I have never felt anything like it, we were absorbed by that marvelous woman—a passionate embrace we'd never dreamed possible. I have the impression that several hours passed until sleep finally overcame us, as if we'd drunk a soporific. It was marvelous, overwhelming, to let yourself fall into that skin as warm and soft as marble. Doctor Sarabia was sweating as he spoke and passed a crumpled handkerchief over his face. We fell asleep in the arms of love, I swear. I swear.

The chill dawn wind woke us—we were cold as ice cubes. In that faint light we looked for the beautiful woman, the object of our delights, but there was no sign of her. We were alone and what's more we were inside a tomb in the old Cemetery of the Plague Victims. So we jumped up at once and saw that there were remains of corpses all around, that we'd been making love, but to the dead. Our fear grew along with disgust at finding ourselves naked and surrounded by the bones and rotted clothing of long dead bodies. Day was dawning and we were shaking not from cold now but from horror. We decided to return to the village together, so great was our fear of what we'd lived through. I am a serious person, all of you know it, a man of science who does not tolerate superstitions. Maybe we drank something at the dinner that clouded our minds and we imagined this whole adventure and the beautiful unknown woman, maybe it's a manifestation of our most hidden desires. If we woke up in the cemetery, it has to have been an effect of the drunkenness. You can see, I've lost my glasses and I'm covered with dirt as if I really had passed the night in a tomb. It has to have been a dream. A dream...

We didn't know how to answer him. Couldn't we go out to the cemetery and see if your glasses are there, suggested Katty. But at the mere mention of a return to the place, the physician and self-proclaimed man of science began trembling like a leaf. No, no, he said, absolutely not.

I only wanted to ask you for a brush to dust off my suit, and the use of a bathroom where I could wash away this pestilent dirt I'm covered with. Doctor Sarabia was whining now, his eyes on my mother, who led him into the house while trying to help him recover from this disturbed state.

We didn't know whether to laugh or ponder. The virtuous doctor running after a lascivious fleshly phantom. What would his wife say? How could he explain himself to her? And the other three drunk on love—where were they? Maybe we should go find them and get them to talk about the beautiful woman who passed by in the moonlight.

After a while my mother came out on the porch a little annoyed that we were laughing so shamelessly at Doctor Sarabia. I can tell he's truly upset, she said, by some terrible experience and he's awfully afraid of what his wife will think when she finds out. I'm going to go talk with her while Guillermo takes the Maestro to see the factory installations. Please entertain Doctor Sarabia and above all try to calm him down.

Our parents waved good-bye and we saw them cross the street. A few minutes later the Maestro and Father left the Sarabias' house and went off in the direction of the dynamite factory, two kilometers away. The wind was beginning to die down and in a couple of hours the deceptive waters of the mirages would appear.

As happens among people who haven't seen one another for many years, our conversation jumped from one subject to another and time passed quickly. Doctor Sarabia joined us and although he remained quiet, he seemed interested and calmer. Three hours later we saw Mother embrace Inés across the street, say good-bye and return home.

Mother smiled placidly. She spoke first to our neighbor, who was now very upset again. Don't worry, my dear Doctor. It seems everybody has spent a rather surprising night, and your wife didn't notice your absence. On the contrary. Due to her piety, she seems to have experienced a miracle. I noticed that my mother was strangely cautious in speaking, but what she said quieted Doctor Sarabia and brought the color back into his face. Be patient and listen to me, my mother advised him. Forget about your dream, Inés is waiting to tell you more important things. The doctor, with his suit brushed clean and his face wearing a smile, bid us good-bye and returned home.

We all have our own dreams, Mother said when he'd left. I'm not a person who believes in painted images, but what Inés has just told me I've never before heard the like of. Maybe her excessive piety makes her see things that the rest of us don't even imagine.

Young and thirsty for adventures, we all urged her to tell us what had happened, the miracle that apparently she'd witnessed or our pious neighbor across the way had told her about. Seeing the expectation in our eyes, Mother asked us to keep completely silent about what Inés had said, since telling it had been a gesture of confidence by our neighbor, and we had to respect every religious belief, even when it came to miracles.

Inés Sarabia, the pious wife of the village doctor, counted among her most precious possessions a painting from Quito which she had inherited from a great-aunt. It was a sort of angel musketeer, life-size, wearing period costume and a hat with a red feather. His complacent face smiled down on the faithful who prayerfully came to ask him for favors and light candles before him. The pious Inés knew little of the history of the painting, but her elderly relatives thought that it was part of the booty brought back by Chilean soldiers after the War of the Pacific. She wasn't sure of anything about it except that it responded miraculously to prayers, a true bridge between her soul and the Almighty.

As was her custom, after the dinner she had shared with us and our distinguished visitors, she returned home, went into her bedroom, and—after her usual washing up—turned to the oratory she had set up in a niche in the wall. There the candles were lit and it seemed to Inés that everything was shining with a brilliance she had never seen before.

On her knees at the prie-dieu, she directed her prayers to the holy angel and noticed that his eyes were following hers, were fixed on her. She redoubled her efforts with great devotion and saw that the entire face now seemed alive, that the red lips were moving as if whispering words and the painted hair was real and shone like silk.

Inés was on the brink of ecstasy! Seemingly her devotion had been rewarded, she would have liked to use a whip to strike herself and do penance, but she was on her knees, absorbed entirely by the murmuring of those lips, so red and sensual, that were whispering words. I am cold, I am cold, the angel kept saying. Inés, come near me, warm me with the heat of your blood. The angel was speaking, was pleading with her for something!

Inés got up and approached the canvas that on this day had come alive, the image that begged for warmth. She felt then that her arms were able to penetrate into the painting's surface and embrace the divine image, which indeed felt cold. Her body united itself with the angel's and her mouth opened to the red lips that asked for warmth. The angel's arms held her as her husband's had never done and she felt that her clothes were falling away, were no longer necessary. An ardor new to her overpowered her senses. She had to warm the angel. As in a dream she saw herself laid on the bed and possessed by that all-powerful being who had granted her the grace of hearing her prayers. The idea of time was erased from her mind: maybe the miracle so often hoped for had occurred. But she was uncertain whether this was a holy event that had embraced her body and made it burn hour after hour that night. A miracle. It must be a miracle. All night her devotion kept her praying, imploring, warming with the heat of her naked body the cold mystery of the holy one, who penetrated her, obliging her to accept with humility her condition as woman. And what a marvelous messenger had come to her! The impossible was promised to her in his words surrounded by music.

You will have three children! Before three days have passed, you will have three children! A miracle!

Do we have the right to refuse the impossible? Inés had asked my mother amid her tears of joy. I believe in miracles, Señora Rosa. I believe, you know I do. It must be a message from heaven.

When I woke up this morning everything in the room was in confusion. I don't know where my husband is. I've looked at the picture, there it is, you can see for yourself. It's returned to its customary serene expression. Poor little one, suffering from cold! I feel filled with joy. What the angel said will be accomplished, I'm certain. It must be a miracle. Señora Rosa, help me not to lose sight of my devotion. I want a miracle! I want...

My mother had listened to this account for three hours and didn't really know what to think. Why would an angel strip the clothes off a woman? Why turn everything in the room upside down? Our neighbor had not gone crazy or anything like that, but there was something about her, something in her femininity, her character as a woman, that had changed during the night.

We listened astonished to the story of Doña Inés Sarabia. The pious lady, had she been seduced by an angel? We all felt the need to drink a double lemonade. As we looked from the porch, every mirage seemed to fall apart; they were out there, it was just a question of making a decision and holding on to them.

When the direction of the wind changed, things would be different.

The evening would come, that rumor of sands, that lament.

The Ivory Moon

When the wind began to die down, we went out to the village's central square, a large area covered with trees and flowers and surrounded by a cement walk along which wooden benches were set at intervals. There we sat down to talk. We needed to comment, each from his or her own viewpoint, on the morning's events. We didn't know what to think of the Sarabias' marriage, the two of them always so concerned about their mutual devotion. And the stories they had told! They seemed incredible to us, to the point that Carlos proposed we go out to the Cemetery of the Plague Victims; decades have passed, he said, we won't get infected. And maybe we can see if what the doctor told us is true. Though we were curious, we said no. The cemetery had been abandoned for almost a century and who knew what surprise we might meet. Besides, we had promised Mother to be discreet about all we had heard.

It's true, Katty said, that things aren't always the way we think they are. There's the façade, and the reality can be quite different. We agreed, although we mocked at her serious tone. She was not moved by our irony and kept insisting that reality can be "different." Look, she said, there's Valenzuela going home and his wife coming out to meet him. You'd think everything's in the good order we see there, but the woman herself told me something else. She's one of two sisters and when Valenzuela went to her parents' house and asked her to marry him and come here to live, she agreed eagerly and they had a few very happy months. Then, a little more than a year ago, Valenzuela started saying that the housework was too much for one person and suggested maybe her sister Julia could come to help her with it. Valenzuela's idea somehow seemed reasonable, even though it included his buying a large mirror to decorate their bedroom. Julia, he said, would sleep in the room next-door; they had thick alpaca covers for her, surely she'd find many pleasures in this new life.

But after the first several nights, Valenzuela insisted on bringing his sister-in-law into the bedroom and sleeping with her. His wife, meanwhile, he relegated to a straw mattress under the bed. From there, he explained to her, she'd be able to see in the mirror how he made love with her sister. Why did the two of them submit to his will? Neither could explain it. They endured this state of affairs without knowing from night to night which of them would sleep in the bed and which on the straw mattress, looking at and listening to the love play up above.

Katty grew excited as she spoke: she couldn't grasp the feelings of each person in this trio. I told her that for Muslims it was permissible to take four women as legal wives and have mistresses as well. All occupied the same house and together reared the children who almost always multiplied miraculously.

It's one thing to know it, Katty said, and another to accept it. Remember that we live in Río Loa. I had to agree, even if for me this place had always been "the station of dreams." After a while we decided to return home and on the way met Juan Siglic, a Yugoslavian immigrant who ran the store that provided the villagers with groceries, fruit and all the housewares they could imagine. He was a kindly, vibrant man, married to a girl also of Slavic origin, a very quiet, timid, painfully thin girl whom the whole village referred to as "the scared rabbit."

At home we rested from the afternoon heat and waited for Father, whom we were expecting home soon with the three visitors. Before long they pulled up in those enormous old green cars. Along with our guests Father had also brought José Kruger and Gustavo Schutt, longtime friends of the family. Since the house seemed small for such a crowd, the Maestro asked Father if it had ever occurred to him to move back one of the walls, saying this method of building had been developed two centuries ago and that certainly one of our walls must have hidden ball bearings. So it turned out. The Maestro pushed the wall slowly open and Asmodeus, always courteous to the ladies, asked Mother not to worry about household tasks since he was there and would take care of any little things needing attention. From the cars he brought in two boxes and spread a folding table with delicacies. By now the space seemed so changed it was more like a theater stage.

Helena Ferrucchi and the Maestro had acquired the practices of nomadic peoples, whom they had doubtless encountered in their travels, and their stories at table endlessly diverted the listeners. All was unfolding in the most normal way, as it does when dear old friends get together. The Maestro, who had fallen somewhat silent, looked out one of the windows and touching my shoulder said: The ivory moon is rising. In a few minutes everything will be possible.

I've missed you—haven't seen you for hours, I told him. He laughed. I'm always there in that shadow chamber, your heart. And don't miss things, think about living every passing moment. I laughed too, feeling his hand on my shoulder; maybe everything was possible, just as I had dreamed so many times.

The other invitees were now arriving. There were our friends, Juan Siglic, Doctor and Señora Sarabia, the Rossos, and my teacher Zoila Campana, all full of delight at the chance to talk and enjoy an intimate get-together with us and our guests. On the other side of the room was Doña Elzira, the trapeze artist, wearing a green velvet cape. She greeted me, just as in the old days, with childlike gestures.

As I gazed and gazed again with overwhelming affection at my family and old friends, I heard a bell ring with a crystal sound, and in its ringing a voice said, "Sit down, the banquet begins now that all have arrived." We sat down at once on high-backed chairs, Helena Ferrucchi on my left and the Maestro on my right. Asmodeus moved around the table as if giving orders to invisible beings who filled the glasses, served the food, and brought in strange objects to make the participants delight and dream.

Soon every diner was involved in passionate conversation with his or her neighbors, laughing and enjoying the event. In the background sweet music seemed to come from within the walls. Who was playing in there? This was no time to worry about trivialities. I reveled in the companionship of the people I loved, toasting the joy of life.

While we were eating, a fold of Helena Ferrucchi's skirt touched my leg and as if by some animal instinct wrapped itself around one of my knees, which seemed to catch fire. Helena, I said to her, some other time I'll tell you how I was once taken prisoner by a desert she-devil; there's too much of a crowd here and they'd envy me so much it would spoil the harmony. Helena laughed. My passion is flesh and blood, she said. You'll remember me the rest of your life.

The conversation and drinking around us were more excited now even than at the start of the evening. Asmodeus could certainly congratulate himself on his success: pleasure was boiling like a vapor above the glasses, giving everybody feelings of inexpressible joy.

Over dessert my father spoke from across the table to remind me of a childhood passion. We know your weaknesses, he said, and that's why we've invited our gentle Elzira, who remembers you with fondness—so you can see the image that used to obsess you one more time. He asked all the guests to move their plates a hand's width toward the center of the table to give the skilled acrobat room to maneuver. Everyone applauded. I watched as, on the other side of the dining room, Elzira removed her cape and, dressed in a minuscule costume of faded green, jumped through a hoop while humming a tune. When she moved along the table's edge in front of us, we could see how expert she was, tumbling through hoops she now kept in motion or, arched over backwards, giving each person a flower she held between her teeth. It was different with me: she kissed me on the mouth. As a child I had looked on ecstatically at these tricks; I had not thought I would ever see them repeated.

This is the reward for your devotion, Helena whispered at my side: I felt my knee burn again as I laughed like someone sharing a secret. There's a time of life when one really is innocent, I said.

We wanted, my father then went on, to give you another gift you'd have appreciated, but though we looked all day we couldn't find an armadillo of the sort we know you like so much. But since it was a gift all the people of Río Loa wanted to give you, our good friend Maestro Leonardo has obtained one for us—and what's more, this one will follow you everywhere.

I saw a small animal covered with scales and reddish fur running across the table. It came up and greeted me solemnly, showing little metal-colored teeth when it spoke. I laughed with delight. Pressing the Maestro's arm, I said: This truly is a celebration of my childhood. I don't know how to thank you and everyone here. He rubbed his hands together as a magician does after performing a trick. Don't treat this too off-handedly, he said. It's the "armadillo with golden teeth," patron deity of the translators of antiquity; it will accompany you for the rest of your life, for it understands and speaks every language. We know that fashionable mechanical toys don't please you, so we've selected a linguist of complete reliability who can transcribe your writings into any language whatever. Besides, my friend continued with malice, arching his eyebrows, it belongs to an extinct species and won't upset you the way a beautiful secretary would.

Seeing my delight and confusion, everyone laughed. At the same moment I felt the small, precious armadillo find its place and brush up against my left foot. The two gifts had further enlivened the general tone of the gathering and everyone was enjoying this rare night of marvels.

Asmodeus then brought in a filigreed ivory glass, in the depths of which bubbled a liquor that smelled of almonds. He let it go and it levitated over the table, at which the Maestro announced: The one whose lips the ivory glass touches will drink its contents and be empowered to tell us a story known to no one. There was prolonged applause. The glass moved along the table and for a moment I believed it would brush Father's lips, but that wasn't to be. Instead it glided to the smiling mouth of our friend José Kruger.

A little surprised it would fall to him to tell a story, our good neighbor took the delicate object and drank the musty wine it held. We hung on his every gesture. It seemed to us that he caressed the ivory before setting it delicately on the table. That same instant we saw him extend both arms and let his head fall forward as if suddenly overcome by sleep. Then a moment later he sat up again and began to talk.

"As you all know, I'm a German, born thirty-six years ago in the outskirts of Hamburg. I lost my father while I was in my teens, and my mother thought I might have a future as a sailor, since I'd always been interested in ships and the sea. So I spent three years in a school for cabin boys that still employed the severe discipline once the rule on sailing ships. My last voyage in the training course was to Africa, where we met many different sorts of people. The Congo above all was strange to me; the Belgians ruled there at the time and the major export product was peanuts, which were peeled and packed into huge baskets as tall as a man. It was there in the Congo that I first experienced a woman's caresses, and so it was there too that I had the first complications of my life. I was passionate, as inexperienced young men often are, and Agar and I—Agar was her name—thought she could hide in one of those large containers and come with us to Europe. My friends prepared a special basket with water and food for the trip, in case something happened to prevent us taking her out of the hold. But destiny deals different cards and though we had no problems in bringing her aboard with the cargo of peanuts, it was days between the ship's departure and our first chance to get down to where we'd hidden the woman.

Before going on, I should tell you that in those days Congolese girls used to cover their bodies with a mixture of honey and palm juice, thinking this would make them more desirable. Many days had passed but we weren't worried since we'd provided her with water and food for two weeks. The only thing that might be hard on her was the strong basket that concealed her but at the same time was a sort of prison.

When we went down into the hold everything seemed fine. We ran to where we knew the baskets were stacked so we could free our friend. But despite our cries we got no answer. We heaved away a few of the baskets and were terrified by the acrid smell we now perceived and giant ants in great numbers that went swarming over the cargo.

Without much effort we were able to pry the cover off Agar's hiding place, only to see with horror that the lovely girl was a skeleton in rags. The honey she had rubbed onto her body had attracted the ants that are so abundant in those regions. We could see that she had tried to get out of the basket, to escape the horrifying end that had come to her in the darkness of the hold. Maybe she had cried out but the sounds of the sea muffled her screams. I collapsed at the side of those rotting yet beloved bones. What could we do? We couldn't hide what had happened for long; we had to tell the captain.

He went down into the hold and with a disgust he could not disguise ordered us to return the bones to the basket and carry them up on deck. We're already at the canal, he told us, this could mean jail for all of you. He was furious at our ignorance, our failure to understand that life has many separate facets. Now it would be necessary to put the remains, with some iron bars to serve as ballast, into a canvas bag that would sink easily. You, Kruger! You slept with her, this was probably your idea. Take her in your arms and throw her into the sea. I was shaking. There was a storm threatening that night. The captain's order was final. If you don't do it immediately, I'll put you into the bag along with her—I don't want any trouble with the port authorities. So I went to the edge of the deck, near the aft anchor, and dropped overboard the sack that held such a precious part of my life. I felt a violent shivering overwhelm me, as though it were winter, and I lost consciousness.

I spent the rest of the voyage seemingly suspended between death and life. An undiagnosed fever oppressed me, and one day I woke up in a hospital for sailors in Hamburg. There the captain visited me and said: What's bothering you? The sea's a womb every good sailor goes back to. Forget the past. We'll all meet again in the other world.

Slowly I recuperated, once more I felt blood running through my veins in an impetuous spate. After three weeks the doctor discharged me. I've spoken with your captain, he said. It's possible these fever fantasies will recur: if so, take quinine, it may alleviate them. That same evening I shipped on another vessel: destination, Hong Kong. Hamburg fell behind, with its thousands of lights and maybe my guilt too. I didn't know when I'd return; the sky was sealed as though with lead, and there were no guiding stars."

Kruger slumped again toward the table and his head almost struck the silverware. Then he jerked awake, obviously confused about what had been going on. We watched him curiously: it appeared he could remember nothing.

The Maestro turned to him and said: Keep the cup as a memento of Africa. Sometimes the moon shines so bright that pain sprouts in the soul. It's a good thing to bring to light the fruits that torment us. Every time you fill this cup with red wine, this storytelling is what will happen.

Asmodeus replenished our glasses and we raised a toast in silence. By the breasts of the moon, offered Juan Siglic from across the table. By the milk that drips from the night, answered the rest of us. The black sorrow of what we had just heard was dissolving into syllables, was being dragged away and scattered by the wind and dust that always intone old songs mistaken by skeptical and ignorant persons for laments.

Shadows on the Sand

Despite the toasts, melancholy hung in the air. Kruger's story had powerfully impressed itself on all our minds. Oblivion, the Maestro said in a light tone, is only an illusion, every action is eternally present. And memory, although the poets try to do some rewiring, is sadly like an invisible wound. He turned in my direction, seeming to indicate me by the gesture, and unable to control myself, I asked Kruger for the ivory glass, poured some red wine, and began to sip slowly.

A heaviness possessed me; the people on all sides had disappeared and I found myself in entirely different surroundings. I suppose that then my head too dropped on the table.

"I find myself next to a woman whose green silk dress clings tightly to her body. It has diagonal stripes over which other pieces of cloth, bright red, have been added. From these stripes hang long fringes covered with metal bells; every movement produces a musical sound. The woman turns and I realize that it is Susana, filled with childlike glee. I've tried it out, she tells me, and this costume produces music that corresponds to the deepest instincts of the self. We laugh like teenagers with a new toy, and begin to explore the immense building where Susana found the costume. The walls surprise us by their lack of all ornament; they are covered with gray oil paint that strikes us as disagreeable. There are no windows and it seems the place is below ground. A man in shirt-sleeves comes from a corridor on the right, full of stained-glass win-

dows, and passes by us. It's Arturo Villalobos, Yolanda's lover, I tell myself. I think of his consuming jealousy and the cruel spirit that at times shone from him. I follow him through a narrow passage and catch sight of him below me in a subterranean stage set of shifting boards and building materials.

From my vantage, I realize, it is easy to throw bits of wood at him, although they do not reach their mark. Then I take a large plum tree branch, go down, and strike him violently on the head, saying, "Bastard! You bastard!" He tries to defend himself and I see that at each blow of mine the branch begins to flower. I suffer a terrible attack of conscience. In a flash, my mind grasps the scene at last: this man died far away many years ago. He bore me a grudge because of my relationship with his lover, but now he has come here to be reconciled with me. His soul in torment wants peace again on this subterranean stage and that is why the plum tree branch is blooming. Disturbed, I think of those bygone years and the follies I committed out of desire. Maybe Arturo never would find peace until I reconciled myself with his soul."

I felt myself waking up at the table, around me a ring of faces, each watching me as if to ask something. I looked at my hand: I was not holding the glass I had drunk from a moment ago. Rather, a small plum tree branch in bloom winked between my fingers.

I smiled at Helena Ferrucchi, who was gazing at me in surprise. I handed her the branch and said, "In memory of an impossible love, and how the ladies torment us men."

I saw that my family and friends had recovered their spirits and so I proposed a new toast. I have old debts to the Maestro, I said, who's assigned me works I thought beyond my powers. He's had the courtesy to accompany me to Río Loa, so let's drink to him and his companions. We raised our glasses again and it seemed the delightful liquor bubbled and breathed a sort of fog over us. The Maestro sipped from his glass, too, and for once I saw in his melancholy eyes a flash of happiness.

As on other occasions, his fingers were playing with a deck of worn cards bearing intricate etchings. Curious, I asked him: Is this a different sort of Tarot? He smiled: Ludwig, this is the original. With it I've read the destiny of the ancient prophets, and that destiny will repeat itself on these old cards until the end of time. He held a few of them out to me and I saw that the scenes etched on them were changing like faces in a mirror. Having them in my own hands was like playing with burning coals. I looked closer at one of them and, seeing my own face in it, gave it back to the Maestro.

From his place at the table my father suggested that we all take a walk in the moonlight, each of us choosing a partner. All agreed and out we went: in the garden the night was warm and only a light breeze reminded us of the desert wind.

Good manners dictated that I accompany Helena Ferrucchi on this excursion. I proposed that she might like to visit an invisible structure that I had discovered in the desert in dreams, where I had been trapped by the she-devil, or maybe explore in some other direction. I remembered that a few kilometers away there was a house surrounded by trees and fenced in by sheets of metal: the only building remaining from an old saltpeter processing plant named "Chela." The site has been dismantled and if the trees are still alive it is because in the area there is a deep well or "pique" from which water used to be drawn. I told Helena that once I had heard there an underground river running eighty meters below the sand. The place is abandoned and maybe we could find it, since the brightness of this night reveals every detail of the desert. She chose this second option and snapped her fingers to call one of the old green limousines so that we could travel more comfortably.

I picked up the armadillo everyone had presented me and put him in my jacket pocket. You don't have to worry about me, he said, I'll always find a way to be at your side. We got into the immense car and for the first time I noticed that there was no driver, or that he was invisible, and that the vehicle went seemingly of its own accord to whatever destination a passenger desired. In a few minutes we were approaching that spot in the desert where the sign "Chela Office" still stood, and in the distance we could make out a dark mass that had to be the house with trees I had found once years before. We got out of the car and saw that the whole place was surrounded by a wall of metal sheets that might keep us from reaching the well. Helena happily took me by the arm and used one of the rings adorning her hand to draw a line on the metal, which at once opened like a door. We went through and the wall closed up again. Inside there truly was a diminutive park of century-old trees surrounded by flowers and exotic plants. A small house stood in the shadows at the far side of the enclosure and we moved toward it. The gardener who lived here many years ago was named Armando Flores, I told Helena. She nodded. We'll get him to come back, she said, and with one of her rings she knocked on the door. Time passed and then a light came on inside and someone approached the door, although whoever it was seemed terribly afraid to open to strangers.

It's Helena Ferrucchi! Open up! my companion shouted. At once we heard the creaking of old wood and the door began to move. It was the same Armando Flores, but looking like a sleepwalker. I asked Helena what had happened to him and she laughed. Don't you remember how luxuriously his fantasies used to burn? Over there are his faded illusions. She showed me yellowed magazine pages that time had almost erased, from which women, naked and provocative, looked out. Now it falls to him to guard the well; he knows little apart from the useless illusion that women are flesh and blood, she told me. Look at him! That's why he's a sleepwalker. And so he was, though the presence of Helena seemed to upset him to the point of horror.

While we looked around the empty and crumbling house, my friend found a lamp that burned like a huge smoking opal. Here's what we need, she said, let's go to the well. She gestured to the gardener and he seemed to collapse into a mound of dust. The sound of water roaring through mysterious underground tunnels could now be heard. We crossed through a barrier of worm-eaten boards and I saw that a stone stairway descended at the edge of the well mouth. Take the ends of my belt, Helena directed me, so you won't have any of the doubts that trouble those who go down into the underworld. I found that grasping the velvet ribbons of her dress allowed me to look calmly on the steep walls along which we descended and which in the opal's light showed distinct bands of color, like jewels washed by the water we heard nearby.

When finally we arrived at what I had believed was a river, I saw with surprise a dam, part of an immense tunnel system whose walls extended almost beyond our sight into the distance. There were various structures—turbines, rails, walkways for moving along the edge of the rushing water—but not a single human being, though occasionally a shadow glided from one tunnel into another. I was unable to overcome my astonishment, which seemed to amuse Helena.

She said: Do you know that one of these tunnels connects with a crevice on the surface, one you're familiar with, The Eye of the Apache?

I accepted this, since I was seeing one marvel after another. Let's go, Helena suggested, it's been years since I was there, maybe we'll find that things have changed.

We walked down a tunnel. Light floated ahead of us and we could see that the walls shone with glyphs and painted figures, perhaps placed there by the region's ancient inhabitants. I stopped to look at some curious inscriptions, passing my fingertips over them. Within me I sensed the armadillo translating: "Where is the house of light, if he who gives life hides himself?" I looked at the inscription in surprise and interrupted the translation: "But this is part of a Mexican Pre-Columbian text." The little animal snickered at my ignorance. It is a prayer, a supplication that nomadic tribes carried with them, he told me. The mansion of light it mentions is the house of love we all seek.

Helena had gone on a few steps and we ran to catch up. We're near, she told me, we just go up this stairway of green rock and we'll be in The Eye of the Apache. When my father had visited this spot eighty years previously, I recalled, the only inhabitants he had found were a pair of naked lovers. Reading this thought, Helena added, That's how lust always treats its servants. This fissure in the desert is even hotter than its surroundings and it's natural that whoever comes here feels heightened instincts. She turned her face to me, and I saw bright coals burning in her eyes. You have a contract with the Maestro, she said as if reminding herself, otherwise love would waste your bones away to dust. An immense wall of rock now rose up before us: The Eye of the Apache, illuminated by warm moonlight, with its neighboring power generating plant and two or three houses with their greenery luxuriating in the warm air.

We walked all around the place as though exploring the source of a mysterious spring. Then Helena, perhaps tiring, stretched out on a block of stone polished by the wind and many suns. I sat down by her, staring and staring at this landscape etching itself into my mind.

Ludwig, she said to me after a while, I have to tell you a story that pains me. But I don't want my sorrow to afflict you too, so I must ask you to lie down on top of me and devour my tongue.

A powerful trembling, a peremptory desire seemed to surge up within my breast. I felt her warm body under mine and her lips like an abyss in which I saw myself falling. I had her sweet, delicate tongue in my mouth, I feared to bite it, and then the armadillo said to me: Bite and swallow that serpent of love, that extremest heat, and when she's within you she'll be able to tell you in dreams all the disasters of the love that drags her like a mourning ghost through countries and seasons. Then I bit off the tongue and it seemed to me immensely long, full of the deliciousness of innumerable subtle tastes. Helena's eyes were closed and when I had finished swallowing that tongue as smooth as a river, she opened them and said: I am in you now like a torrent of water; if I never looked at you with love before, it was to save you from feeling the terror of these coals burning in my eyes. I hardly heard her,

I was kissing her face that was chilled by the rising breeze. This is con-
fession by the tongue, my lover said then, seemingly full of pain. We
were entwined in silence, and with a gesture she called the car that had
brought us to the well lost in the desert. Still abashed with wonder, we
climbed into the high seats. Then Helena smiled and said: Don't be sad
on my account. I'll be there within you every time you want to bite
your tongue.

Slowly, wrapped in each other's arms, we were carried back to
the village as if mysterious ropes pulled us. It hurt us to separate, to
have to start chatting again with the other couples engaged in nocturnal
expeditions, to listen to the usual jokes, and laugh.

It was long past midnight when Father decided it was time to
take our guests to their lodgings. As on the previous night, we were
singing and telling stories, entertaining ourselves with comments. We
left Helena and Asmodeus at the guest hostel and Father took the Maes-
tro to the Sarabias'.

On the way home, my sisters were talking with José Kruger and
Gustavo Schutt, while Carlos and I exchanged opinions a block or so
behind them. My brother, always so jovial and friendly, had hardly said
a word as we went along until, grabbing hold of my arm, his voice full
of emotion, he began telling me certain memories he had from the pre-
vious night, memories of things, he said, that had touched him inwardly.

*I don't know what to think about all this, he said by way of intro-
duction.*

*"Last night I found myself in a circle made up of a varied group
of persons, and how we had gotten there none of us seemed to know.
The physical surroundings are like an immense treeless inner court-
yard. Also, I have the impression in this dreamlike state that it is winter
and everything is covered with snow. In the center of the courtyard,
surrounded by large rocks, is a mountain of sand which, on closer ex-
amination, proves to be salt.*

*There are eight or ten of us in the circle. At times those who
arrive are welcomed, 'initiated,' and at times not, since the ritual is so
complicated that no one succeeds in completing its final stages. Then a
stranger appears and the people in the circle retire into the building. It is
thought, I believe, that some error has been committed and I almost
fear that the new arrival is going to be flung into the mound of salt as
into a swimming pool. But this does not happen and along with two*

other people I withdraw with the stranger to a room inside the building. Then he is asked many questions, some of them quite unusual. I see that the man being questioned is one of the household. 'If the destiny of XX depends on this,' he says, 'he does not wish to live in such a way.'

He pushes back a sort of monk's cowl and shows us his head crosshatched by many twists of hair. Then I realize that the place is a lamasery, and that in some way all actions here have a magic effect that changes the universe. Seemingly, after the interrogation, the stranger is accepted.

Then a woman with a little boy comes in. The boy, five or six years old, has been accepted already and plays in the salt garden. He has been called to entertain and be a companion to the Dalai Lama, who himself is a child of that age. I look at the little boy and then at the monk, associating them in my mind with your son, Javier. I see that it falls to me to interview the boy's mother. You will be able to speak with her, they tell me, she speaks French. As I prepare to launch a conversation of questions and answers with the woman, under a tree with many branches I see Father, smiling warmly as always and wearing an immense straw hat to protect himself from the sun. I approach and greet him, trying to explain that this place is a convent, magic, dangerous.

He looks at me imperturbably, but knowing I have omitted something, he goes directly to the Prior. When has he ever feared anything? I say to myself. I see him later inside one of the rooms of the vast building tied to a bed and at his feet an important inquisitor, a monk of the highest rank in the hierarchy. Contacts are mentioned, and I sense that the people in question are Lieberman, of the Museum of Modern Art, and a gracious woman whom I met and talked with many years ago. The inquisitor, with his feet scarcely touching the ground, bends over the bed and, joining his lips to my father's, says: 'Only one head, only one language.' By saying this he levitates my father's body, which is rigid, into an upright position. Later the two of them laugh together, Father and the inquisitor, who says to him: Your sons don't realize that this can be done. They go on laughing and joking, which calms me and makes me feel happy."

My brother seemed relieved after telling me these dream adventures of the night before. As we embraced I put a word in his ear: We're called to live experiences more mysterious than anything we imagine. He nodded. We had arrived at our porch and the flowers breathed a perfume that invited us to dream. Tomorrow we'll see where all this leads us, I said. Maybe dream is only a parallel world whose first outlines we can barely make out.

I had trouble going to sleep; strong feelings and the long underground journey still affected me. Even the cool moonless night could not make me forget all I had lived through in the last few hours. I settled myself between those alpaca blankets I had not felt since childhood and at last sank into the interior of my being.

Two Cards and a Miracle

I woke to the rooster's crowing, a little before dawn.

I felt extraordinarily rested, in possession of an energy I hadn't known for years. Cold water in the washbasin drove away the last languor from me; I heard coughing on the porch, so I went out and discovered Gustavo who, seated next to the empty hammock, was looking toward the coming of dawn with worried eyes.

I greeted him with a smile and asked, How about some strong black coffee? He said yes, and when in a few minutes I brought him the steaming cup, he added: Thanks. Maybe this will help me forget the bad dreams I've had.

Why? Better if you tell me your dreams, I said. That'll get the weight of their wings off you. He was gloomy and tired, as if he had spent the whole night awake. An old friend of my parents, Gustavo Schutt came from a Hanover family, and I had often looked at his photographs of his mother and sisters in front of their old ancestral home. He had studied medicine in accord with his parents' wishes but had abandoned what promised to be a brilliant career to pursue a cabaret singer who, after a few weeks, had deserted him. He was in Kiel at the time, so it was easy to get a job as a medic on one of the many ships in the bay and set off to see a bit of the world. He had been traveling a few months when chance prompted him to leave the ship at Antofagasta, Chile's principal export point for metal and saltpeter.

How did he and Father meet? Neither of them could remember, but it wasn't hard to guess that it had been at one of those parties where destiny brings together the most disparate crowd, drawn by drink and the unchanging lure of feminine charms.

At the port Gustavo lived with, or maybe he married, a sensual mulatto woman named Sara. The adage that opposites attract was to some extent realized in their union. Sara, a little more than thirty years old, was a constant temptation to every man who passed through the place; her character, powerful and lascivious, was of a piece with her primitive beauty, an inheritance from an African grandmother. She got on well with Gustavo, who was tolerant, even blind, to his wife's defects and weaknesses. Along with Sara came her mother, who for years had menaced every person she saw with her certainty that at any moment she was going to drop dead. But all this didn't seem to bother Gustavo who, perhaps, grew used to putting up with the personalities of the two women. On the contrary: any day of the year we might see him walk by our house, dressed in a pristine white suit, his handsome face adorned with a mustache as blond as his hair, with his never-absent mandolin under his arm.

But now he seemed a victim of some terrible worry and even after two cups of coffee I wasn't able to get from him one word about what had happened the night before. I saw his mandolin leaning in a corner, and decided to walk down to the general store. Then I heard him murmur: "Don't go. I have something very strange, very important, to tell you." I pulled my chair up to the hammock and settled down to hear what was bothering him.

Last night, he said, while we were strolling in the moonlight, your distinguished friend joined us. I was curious and asked him about the playing cards I saw him turning over and over between his fingers; generously he handed me two cards which, he said, would satisfy my curiosity. I don't know if you've seen them, they're thick parchment with old tinted woodcuts printed on them, or so I thought at first. We were chatting with your mother so I put the two cards in my pocket. In the brilliant moonlight our walk was enchanting and the four or five of us who were together had a most entertaining evening, sharing memories and trading tales of our adventures. Then—after you and I and your sisters and Carlos returned from walking the visitors over to the guest hostel—your father invited me to sleep here at your house, in the hammock, as I've done before.

All was in darkness and I had fallen asleep, or so I believed, for I found myself deciding—guided by some secret impulse—to examine the old playing cards. Although everything, as I said, was dark, they were shining as if phosphorescent. One of them seemed rather familiar; then the tinted engraving came alive and showed itself to be the house where I lived in childhood with my grandparents. Suddenly I saw some blackbirds circling over the granary and one of my sisters, crying, told me of the bitterness my dead mother felt toward me precisely because I had been one of her favorite children. Later I saw her, an old woman dressed in a pristine black suit; opening her eyes, she looked at me intensely, as if knotted up with sorrow. She didn't scold me for what I'd done, which might have given me some relief, but instead, with the awful smile of the dead fixed on her lips, she said to me that one of the witches I was living with would abandon me forever. Then she lifted her hand in the gesture of dismissal used when an interrogation has been ended and the guilty party can leave.

I fear, my dear Ludwig, that this vision of my dead mother presages some terrible event. You know very well that I'm anchored in this village by my love, my passion for Sara, despite all her faults. I'm afraid for her. I know that her mother, if she could, would have already made Sara vanish from my arms.

I didn't know very well how to comfort him. I asked if he had talked with Sara and he admitted that fear had kept him away from his own house; passion can have such a dominating effect on some people. But it's only a card! I said to him, without much conviction. Besides, you can consult the Maestro about its meaning, since he's read the cards for many years. If you want me to, I'll talk to him myself.

The worry did not disappear from our friend's face, which was even more pallid now in the first rays of the sun. The other card your friend lent me is even worse—I suppose he must be a wizard. On it I saw an ancient, desolate landscape, but looking more closely I recognized it was our own Río Loa dynamite factory at night. I could distinguish each building your father had constructed, the tall lead towers, the reinforced structures buried in the sand, the silent smooth-running carts that carry the explosives. Suddenly, I saw one building after another blow up, and all the details of the place, even the walls themselves, were lit as though by a nighttime fireworks display. It was a disaster, a tragedy for all of us. The same blackbirds I had seen circling in the other card now descended from the sky and drew my attention to a series of faces, those who were going to die. I managed to recognize among them Gaona and Villavicencio; the others were strangers, but each one's forehead bore the same red mark. Just like the first card, this one makes me feel some catastrophe must be about to descend on us. I

43

tell you I'm afraid. Even talking about it makes me shake.

I gave him a friendly hug, saying he shouldn't worry about it anymore, that we'd be careful. The first thing to do was to get him some food and then he could rest. I would return the playing cards to the Maestro and ask him to explain the visions. Gustavo Schutt seemed relieved. From inside the house my mother called us to breakfast.

The joy that seems a quality of youth was evident in that breakfast shared with my brother and sisters. All of us wanted to talk at once, laughing and making affectionate jokes. Mother laughed too to see us, and Gustavo, who had been so anguished a few hours before, seemed somewhat more serene.

My sister Ida asserted passionately that love works miracles. She strongly maintained that from the bottomless depths of feelings the strangest flowers can bloom. Playing devil's advocate, we offered all sorts of ridiculous arguments against her, delighting in the dispute for its own sake while understanding that all of us shared the sentiment in our hearts.

We still hadn't finished enjoying Mother's raisin cake when there was a knocking at the door and Doctor Sarabia burst in, almost beside himself with worry. Señora Rosa, he said to Mother, please, you must come with me. Inés is sick and I think your help is absolutely necessary. All of us offered to come as well, but he said no, that only someone with experience could assist him in the matter. My mother got ready to leave at once and the rest of us, staying behind, were resentful that he didn't consider us grown-up and worthy of his respect. We got our own back by making fun of the rush he was in, as if it were some life-or-death situation.

He seemed deaf to our mockery, and taking my mother's arm, went across the street almost at a run.

He must have found a treasure, Kuni hissed beside me. Maybe he's stunned and won't invite us over because he doesn't want to share his precious jewels with young people like us.

Then Father went by in one of the factory trucks and, seeing Gustavo, offered to take him home. He accepted and we saw them disappear in a cloud of dust.

The next hour passed in laughter, narrating minor affairs we all knew about, Río Loa being such a small village. The night before, Sixto Lora, one of the dynamite factory employees, had talked to Juan Siglic, and Juan had assured him that the following day—today—in the evening he, Juan, would host a small party, now that Elvira Ossorio, whom Sixto had courted for so many years, had at last accepted his proposals. Sixto was happy, although the preparation time that had been set by his fiancée seemed much too short. But since he was afraid that her acceptance was due only to the unaccustomed joy of the last few days, he had thought it best to raise no objections but take advantage of the fair wind that now drove the heart of the beautiful Elvira toward his desires. Juan Siglic promised to give Sixto everything necessary for the party. It should be modest, he suggested, since there's no time left for anyone in the village to get you the gifts that love, of whatever type, truly merits.

Ida, Katty and Kuni took this news as a confirmation of what we had been saying earlier. Almighty love was able to break down any barrier. Carlos and I were more skeptical, we would have liked to ask Father why the wedding ceremony had to be so hurried—something about which we had received no information. He was fond of Elvira, and although he was discreet, maybe he would explain it to us when he returned home.

Ida, on the other hand, in love with love, reminded us that the beautiful Virginia, who everyone thought had no weaknesses, left her parents' house when it was least expected with the man of her dreams who, since he had no horse, had abducted her on a humble bicycle. All of us knew this was true, but what we were not sure of was whether we would be invited to this wedding that was going ahead in only twenty-four hours. Would they be married in a civil ceremony? Would the priest come from Calama? Would they invite the famous Father Del Valle from Chuquicamata?

We all laughed as we imagined the various possibilities, especially that the famous priest of Chuquicamata might come. The whole village knew that he, despite his vow of chastity, lived at Marina Valdenegro's and that her two children were not born out of acts of devotion, but were his. Maybe Marina's beauty and youth had seduced the poor cleric, but there was not a woman in all the settlements and oases within a hundred-kilometer radius who did not look at her suspiciously, blaming her control of him on witchcraft—all of which made her even more mysterious and seductive.

Meanwhile we saw the tailor Modesto Sotomayor and his assistant run toward the Sarabia house. Why had they been called? Weren't we more adult and trustworthy than the assistant, a man who was at all times chained to his sewing machine?

Let's go for a walk to the river, I suggested to Carlos and our sisters. All the people here seem so wrapped up in their affairs—let's have some fun, go swimming in the pools where the river's warm and the air is cool. Let's walk toward the fields, which are radiantly green near the river bank; maybe we could go even farther, reach the cliffs honeycombed with tombs that rise up along the river. All of us eagerly set out on the excursion.

As we walked, laughing and singing old songs, we passed an ancient adobe wall and saw that the ground behind it was swept completely clean and four posts had been driven to form a square two meters on a side. So, said Carlos, it looks like tonight Sofía the medium will fall into a trance and everybody round about will come to consult her about the dead. We knew he was right. Within the square marked out by the four posts, a smaller circle, painted red, had been traced in the dirt and we understood what it signified. It was a ceremony we had seen many times, and though this reminder of the dead sobered us a little, we continued on our walk, maybe attempting to forget.

Two kilometers farther down, the river runs between high cliffs, and the stones on the river bottom, polished by the current, form natural bathing pools where the water is transparent. We plunged in there, prospecting for the time outside time where dreaming and living are synonyms.

After a while Carlos got out of the water and started to climb one of the cliffs above the river. We knew it was dangerous but that there is also a special kind of temptation in it. He quickly reached one of the openings in the rock and in a moment called out to us and held up a trophy. We knew without going up that he had entered a "gentilar," as those burial sites of the ancient inhabitants are called; besides, we did not want to leave the warm placidity of the water. My brother resigned himself to our inertia and came down carrying in his bag the two objects he had shown us from a distance: a skull devoid of all flesh, and a little figure made of black pottery, half animal, half human. He handed it to me because I looked interested. Blow into it, he commanded, it's a "demon-lament." I obeyed and a long moan seemed to echo through the stone caverns all along the river.

Our sisters were upset. Why this lament? they demanded. Besides, Father's told all the villagers it's wrong to dig around in the tombs. We knew it. Somehow noon had arrived: it was time to go back home, but Carlos and I could not resign ourselves to giving up our treasures. My brother murmured in my ear: We can talk to this dead man tonight if we put his head in front of the medium. The idea enthused me and scared me at the same time.

Slowly, unwillingly, we returned. It was hot and we thought it would be pleasant to be already sitting on the porch by the time the mirages began to appear. We walked faster and soon were at the house, that house each one of us remembers vividly.

My beloved sister Kuni took my arm and whispered: "Are you still afraid of the night, do you still cry when the wind runs through the porches, and can't be heard?" As I listened, her words seemed as familiar to me as the lyrics of an old song.

When we got to the porch, which was covered with nasturtium petals, my mother came out to meet us. She seemed upset; something was worrying her. I have to talk to you all, she said. Things have happened that I can't explain. I went with Doctor Sarabia, who said Inés was sick. I'd seen her only the night before, and thought some of the food might have disagreed with her. The doctor couldn't tell me anything.

When we entered her room, I saw her in bed, surrounded by pillows. Taking my hand as if she wanted to tell me a secret, she said, Señora Rosa, I am sure I'm about to give birth. She pushed aside the pillows and blankets and I saw that in fact her abdomen was swollen, so much so that I couldn't understand how it could have happened in such a short time—the day Ludwig arrived she seemed perfectly normal. The doctor was so upset that he was useless. I asked them to get two large pans of hot water ready for bathing the baby and called on the tailor to prepare the clothing the event requires. I gave birth to all of you—so I understood the problems we were facing. Inés was calm and didn't seem to have pains or contractions, though her belly was visibly swelling before my very eyes to such a size that I began to fear it would burst open.

It's a miracle, Señora Rosa, said the mother-to-be. The angel who was with me two days ago whispered: "Within three days you will give birth to my children." I saw that she was looking at the painting on the wall: the figure seemed to live and move in his own world, all the while mocking us.

The moment arrived when Inés' womb had swollen to such a point that her sex looked more like a door surrounded by hair. Suddenly I saw this door begin to open and, like something coming from a soundless depth, the head of a boy, five or six years old, began to emerge. He slid out very quickly; his hair was red and he was perfectly dressed in a black velvet suit with red lapels. He seemed to be pulling on a rope with his little hands and while he was doing this, he turned to us and greeted us courteously in correct adult speech, as if he had always known it, and said: Dear ladies, have no fear about this, now that we are finally born of woman. Wait a bit so that I can pull on this cord and bring out my sisters. As we struggled to overcome our enormous astonishment, we saw two more creatures, more or less the same age as the boy, emerge from Inés' sex-door. They were girls dressed in violet whose expressions were direct, even provocative. Then the three took up places next to the bed, their clothing perfectly arranged, as if they had stepped from a dream, and they greeted us with laughter and spoke to Inés. You are our mother, and so that the rite may be completed, allow Señora Rosa to squeeze your breasts and fill some cups with your milk. If we suckled directly, we would bite off your nipples.

My mother, despite her fear, had then proceeded to massage Inés' breasts, and two jets of milk had directed themselves into two jars. How repulsive to submit to the animality of human beings! the boy cried with clenched teeth. Turning again to us, he said: Dear ladies, please be assured that you have nothing to worry about from us who are at your service at any time you wish. Permit me to introduce myself. My name is Gaspar, and for this reason people often have confused me with the Chaldean magician. My sisters are named Judith and Salome—they can take care of themselves—and after we drink from the milk jars we will stop growing. Actually they were more like miniature adults than children, with their ironies and a knowledge far beyond the capacity of children of five or six. The girls were like small seductive women, cruel and lascivious.

In the midst of our astonishment, my mother said excitedly, in that short time, sudden as an eternity, the newborns had already aged a year or two. They walked around the rooms as if they had lived in the house for years. The one who called himself Gaspar returned to the bed where Inés lay and said to her: Thanks for the shelter of these two nights. Since we wish to show our gratitude, we will put your belly back into place. The three went up to her and pushed against the flaccid abdomen. There, that does it! said Gaspar. And so that no one can ever doubt your virtue, let me place my lips upon your sex, so that you will be virgin forever. After that, they drank the milk with some reluctance, as if it tasted like a medicine.

Once everything he had to say was finished, he saluted us with a laugh. Then, along with his sisters, he bowed to the figure in the painting and they all went out to run around in the village like any other children of their age.

Living Dolls

What Mother told us had made us less fearful than curious, for the pious Señora Sarabia giving birth to some type of adult children was not an everyday sort of thing. We were eating fried swordfish steaks—mother often used to prepare this dish exquisitely, and that very morning we had picked out an albacore from a truck that came from the coast. The conversation was as lively and fascinating as ever, but we were eager for the heat to abate—the heat that made strangers dizzy and created the mirages that always recede, no matter how one longs to reach them.

When the first breeze that announces the evening winds began to blow, we all acted on our shared desire to go through the village and try to catch sight of the three children, Gaspar and his sisters, and form our own impression of what our mother had told us. We tied on our straw hats and went down toward the square. Curiosity spurred us to look high and low, but we found nothing abnormal in the village, and decided to sit down on one of the benches and talk things over. Our sisters thought the best idea was to go visit Inés Sarabia herself and see if anything new had happened since Mother left her. Carlos and I thought it would be better to wait awhile and see how events unfolded. As a last resort, my brother said, we could ask Sofia the medium about it tonight.

At this I recalled the skull he had been carrying around in his bag all that morning. Where'd you leave it, I asked. With a grin he said he'd put it in the last place anyone would think of—the oven. The oven's almost never used and I just want to keep it hidden till tonight.

Engrossed in talk, we had not immediately noticed the shouts and shrieks now coming from behind the school, from near the yard where we had played as children. The school was closed for vacation and so, wondering what could be going on, we walked around to the other side, which formed a shelter against the wind and from which the noises seemed to come. Had some animal injured itself on the fence? Was someone suffering an outrage?

Approaching, we saw that the yard's gate was open and a small girl, elegantly dressed, was walking in and out. We went up to ask her what was going on and she greeted us ceremoniously, like an accomplished actress: We're preparing a little performance for Ludwig, which Maestro Leonardo has charged us with. Take your seats here under the trees: the stage and sets will be ready in a few minutes.

But I've forgotten to introduce myself, she added. My name is Judith. I'll be back right away with some refreshments. We were dumbfounded and had not even thought of introducing ourselves in return. The little girl was truly a diminutive woman, very alluring, dressed with a stylish elegance never seen in our village. Moreover, every single gesture she made was so expertly provocative that it was difficult to get her out of one's mind.

She had disappeared into one of the classrooms and soon we heard a sound of circus music and saw her return accompanied by her two siblings, Salome and Gaspar, who presented themselves with a bow and a curtsey and announced a "little drama with marionettes" entitled "Why Can't Sinners Stand the Truth?"

The miniature actors, so we supposed them, were enchantingly attractive. Gaspar's black suit with red piping gave him the look of an orchestra conductor. His sisters appeared to be consummate ballerinas, Salome melancholic and Judith, whom we had just met, happy and jovial.

They opened before us a sort of wardrobe that could be taken apart and made into a theatrical stage, on which we could see that every detail was perfectly crafted. Judith came to our seats and in a musical voice told me that the pieces would be acted live: they were a gift ordered by Maestro Leonardo so I would not forget that dreams are a different reality in which roles are played and the total fate of existence is thereby confronted.

For our first number, she said, I give you these glasses to protect against the rays of the sun. Many years have gone by and your gaze might melt the actors. We put on the sunglasses, laughing, and saw that a light like that of a solar eclipse now suffused the stage.

May I present, cried Gaspar, an artist you have always wanted to hear. Immediately a figure came forward, about two feet tall and dressed in European clothing of the last century, who bowed and said: I hope this evening gives you the same enjoyment you've always felt in listening to my compositions.

I was bursting with wonder. It was Franz Schubert there on the boards! He himself, and alive! As if reading my thoughts the great musician turned my way with a smile: Sometimes the world above exchanges images with other worlds. In gratitude for your devotion I'm going to play for you tonight "Death and the Maiden." He went to a piano at the rear of the stage; to the rhythm of his music a shy maiden appeared and behind her a dark cavalier who seducingly tried to catch her in his net. Their dance grew ever stormier till at last the cavalier had taken his prey. Leveling death reigned in all its power.

We were living a dream. After the dance had ended, the curtain rose again at our applause and back came the dwarf Franz Schubert. Bowing and smiling, he said particularly to me: Don't worry, we'll meet again in the other world. Truly I could not shake off my amazement, remembering how often in listening to that music I had imagined the marvelous being who had composed it.

You can remove your glasses now, Judith announced. The next piece is set in recent times and you'll be seeing some persons who aren't always agreeable. The length of this one depends on you, and if you want you can join in. Since the characters are low, we've chosen popular music for accompaniment. She bowed and held up a little scene card with phosphorescent lettering: "Any similarity to real persons and events is exactly that."

We heard the music of the Oruro carnival. From the rear of the stage came Gaspar dragging a huge box that looked something like a pigeon coop due to its window-like holes. This fake building stood on four heavy feet and across its façade bore an inscription: "Are the tortures of education mandatory for us all?" I laughed to see this absurd contraption, which reminded me of the long nightmare years I had spent working in the Ministry of Education.

To our surprise the model came to life and with harsh grating noises began to emit smoke from all four sides, like a tiny Chinese dragon. Every discipline leads to fanaticism.

When the smoke cleared we could see running from the building a succession of small dolls, some bald, some with heavily pomaded hair—the various ministers and functionaries were abandoning their office-incubator. Meanwhile, a crowd of children had gathered at the windows and were throwing down stones at these solemn dignitaries.

Suddenly the music grew more strident and a giant bird beak burst from the edifice, striking and swallowing the sordid ministers and secretaries. We now saw the building let out streams of happy children singing burlesque songs. One of them was lighting some papers and the flames rapidly spread and enveloped the grotesque building. A din of fireworks prevented us from making out voices as the pigeon coop-ministry exploded in a veritable pyrotechnic display. The spectacle was unbelievable: desires made real.

Now from the rear of the stage came the sound of a flageolet and several flutes. Slowly, as though levitating through the scene, a tiny woman covered in veils glided forward: It was Salome, the tempting stepdaughter of the Tetrarch of Galilee, and she began to dance before us. We could not utter a word, and felt as though even breathing might interrupt the pure delight of those graceful movements, each more erotic than the last. When we thought we had reached the point where our attention could no longer bear up under the sweet torture of watching those veils blow in the wind, she suddenly stopped and said: Richard Strauss was wrong, the real dance of love is done by the hands. Then we saw her floating before us, head downward, her elastic, lascivious little body covered by a skin of flame and perfume.

When the flute music ceased, we saw her move off like a bird into the depths of the stage. We sat there panting, absolutely overwhelmed by the charms of little Salome. Apparently her perfume had gone to our heads.

I looked at my brother and sisters enjoying this feast mainly of *guignol*, since only Schubert and the lovely Salome could be considered true virtuosi. Behind us the wind was still blowing over the desert, whirling into spirals any dust that had not yet crystallized.

Then Judith emerged and, with a conniving wink, announced the next turn. It will be without background music, she said, so that you can appreciate "Where the Singers Come From." I saw, then, Judith and Salome carrying a woman about two feet tall, like the marionettes we had already seen, and absolutely alive, although her surroundings and our presence made her fearful. This doll was dressed with the garish allure of a prostitute but wore over her clothing a chastity belt that made a rather ridiculous picture.

Here is her ladyship, Salome said to me. I believe she wishes to speak with you. It was Yolanda, a woman who had tortured me a good part of my life. And there she was, alive, with tears pouring from her eyes! She was trying to speak but could not, out of horror.

What do you want! I asked her. Do you know that your former lover came to me to be reconciled? Her eyes were fairly bursting from their sockets.

With a sudden motion Judith and Salome ripped away her dress and she was left clothed only in shreds. Now, her arms bound before her on a small post, I saw her as in the old days, naked and undeniably cruel. There's no key for the chastity belt, the lady teacher has it, Judith and Salome told me; you'll have to open the lock with this little soldering iron. I did not know how. I took the soldering iron—a sort of slender pencil—between my fingers, inserted it into the metal lock, and saw woman and belt suffer an electric shock. It will have to be stronger, said Judith; this is the game that never ends. I plunged the iron deep into the lock and at that moment saw Yolanda opening her legs and changing into a tiny animated skeleton. Every time I removed the iron she turned back into my old torturess who, fate dictated, now had to suffer this torment of the hot iron. I repeated the operation four or five times, body-skeleton-body, until I saw that her tears had become blood-colored. I then commanded the two sisters to take her away and they, seizing her by the arms, dragged her offstage. But immediately they brought her back and said to me that she had one desire: the desire, they said, of a woman possessed.

Alsina! I said. Turn back into the witch you've always been.

At my words I saw her, now tranquil, go off on her own into the depths of the stage.

A few moments later the three siblings reappeared and with huge ostentatious bows thanked us for our presence at their humble entertainment.

On all our behalf I thanked them in return, and requested that any future show should include only such erotic numbers as were banned by the censor; I find all others, I said, unpleasant. Gaspar was cast down by my criticism. I have one more little act, he said, a game of ballistics that might amuse you.

You don't understand me, Gaspar, I said. I've seen that game so many times over the years that it's incomprehensible how you can think to offer it as a novelty. Thanks for the show, we'll see the three of you later, at dinner.

We got up from our seats under the green pepper trees, those marvelous plants with leaves like feathers. By now, as we turned toward home, the wind was scarcely perceptible.

Gaspar, Judith and Salome could, if they really wanted to, be enchanters.

Slowly we trooped back to our house, my brother and sisters making jokes and laughing over the living puppets we had seen. For my part, I felt tired and disgusted, and when we had arrived and greeted Mother, I asked them to excuse me as I wanted to take a short nap: there was a full program that evening and I needed rest. The moment I laid my head on the pillow, I felt dream descend on me like balsam, the dew that renews all things. This dream too brought me other images, perhaps forgotten ones from my own mind.

"It is late. Under a leaden overcast we are walking the high plain that stretches before the house where I live with my parents. As so often before we are taking the route to the volcano Mount Miño. There is a small hollow in the desert earth here, with perhaps a few plants in it. Along with me are some school friends: Ernesto Rosso, Pedro Garzón, and Segundo Santos, the epileptic, who on one occasion had recovered from a seizure in the midst of a wake in his honor.

We are playing with magical whips that have such power they seem to crack themselves. Hissing through the air, they can entwine themselves around people the way snakes do. Each is four or five meters long and about two inches thick and has the color of black coffee. The cloudy sky has turned still more oppressive and all at once I realize that there is a man with me who is going to kill me. First, though, he lets me choose my weapon: a quadrangular machete or a whip. The whips move of their own volition, suspended in the air, and I perceive that somehow they obey me: I make my choice, wrap it around the man threatening me and carry him with me, tied up this way. Now I am sure he can not kill me.

Under the unfailing cloudy light we cross the low hills of the pampa and skirt an immense building, two or three blocks long, made of adobe and whitewashed. Seemingly inside it there is a structure of canes and thick wire that produces the sense of something vast and menacing. What we can see is the structure's wall, which is the exterior wall of a corridor running the entire circumference of the huge building. About twice a man's height, this wall barely lets us glimpse a bit of the interior through arched windows, some mainly bricked in and others entirely so, a fact that bespeaks the place's great age.

Somehow it recalls old saltpeter plants abandoned and sealed up with rusting sheet metal. I see myself suddenly inside this building, or perhaps I had never been outside of it, or perhaps I had walked to my right and I am now in one of its titanic rooms, unfurnished except for an enormous table and two chairs—I am sitting there with a Colombian boy whom I know only slightly. He has with him a manuscript unfolded on the table, bearing very large and rather unusual script, which he tells me is an oration of the prophets that he has to learn. I hear him repeat it loudly a couple of times, to ready himself to pass some difficult test: Either learn English or else go to hell—it seems to me that is what he is saying. He recites word after word and finally, as if he has been proven guilty of an unknown sin, someone comes to get him.

I am alone, I have been left alone. The wind howls and bellows through the rooms, and I start walking again along the corridors, hiding in the angles of their walls. But a spirit-woman finds me and seizes me. She wears a threadbare dress and her disheveled appearance reminds me of certain Tibetans I have seen in photographs. She tells me that once she was Joanne Stranford and lived on Yonge Street, but that now she has caught me and will keep me bound by her powers. I learn something sexual from her, a wisdom or expertise which, I realize in the dream, comes from the devil, for here, in this place, all is demoniacal.

Then I see a couple, very composed, approach us down the corridors, dressed in ochre-colored raincoats as if about to go out, and weeping copiously. The woman tells me her name is Pepa, or Pepis; the man accompanying her—stocky, with an olive complexion—walks like a somnambulist.

Curious, I ask her how he is but she tells me he has been dead a long time. We are moving now along the exterior corridor of the building, and we descend a few steps that lead to the antechamber of a ballroom, where I notice several doormen, solemn as doormen always are. The couple walks on, displaying a ticket, and I come to an employee seated at a little table. Only then do I perceive that this one is an old woman. In my surprise I explain to her that I have been invited but did not know I would need a ticket to enter. This 'ticket' is an eight-letter word, such as 'enfolded,' 'embolism,' 'stopcock.' I understand then that the number of letters does not correspond to that which I had been told, but at this point the woman shows me her kneecaps, to which she gives some other name, and tells me this is the ticket. Maybe I have entered?

I do not know exactly what happens then, I only remember that it is the dead of night and I am walking with some other people down desolate streets, along blank walls of adobe, at the center of a village. The person at my side tells me that there, in the distance, is the devil, that if I would stand on tiptoe I would be able to see his red cape stirring in the wind. I am not certain that it is the devil. We seem to be walking along the outer edge of a place where peoples and landscapes continually replace each other, as though they were only changing illusions and phantasmagoria.

Then I see that I have been charged with arranging paintings in an immense factory, and to do this work I must speak with the personnel directors. There is a nightmare atmosphere, and this task I am so bound up with is a form of slavery I have been subjected to. I come to a small habitation with adobe walls and there I ask a woman dressed in black if I can help her. There is a person there buried head down in the earthen floor—I see only the soles of the feet. The woman notes my horror and orders me peremptorily to clean the grates in the floor through which the heat rises from hell."

Awakening, I hear Mother busy with some other ladies in the kitchen preparing dinner. I go and join them and bask in their warmth and affection, as they gossip about every one of the invitees who will come this evening, when the sun sets and the moon emerges again from the depths of the sand.

Dinner With the Maestro

As I was getting together with my brother and sisters, the postmaster came by to deliver an enormous package addressed to me from Santa Fe, Argentina. It was not heavy enough to contain books, and curiosity spurred us to see what was in it before our guests arrived. With excited delight we unwrapped and opened the mysterious box and found, to our surprise, an enormous rhea egg and a short note from my friend, the poet Enrique Molina, lamenting that I had not been able to come to the conference on Latin American surrealism. He wished me happiness in love and signed himself, above a flourish, Enrique the Uncertain.

We laughed over this piece of whimsy: why had he sent us such a phenomenal ostrich egg? A bright idea, said Ida, of a poet, always ready to remember childhood and live immersed in it.

Mother asked us then to go greet the guests. We went out onto the porch as the enormous automobiles bringing them drew up. Father and the Maestro were talking animatedly in a language that had died out in Borneo at the end of the last century. The lovely Helena wore a brilliantly colored gown and was escorted by the now very ceremonious Gaspar, Judith and Salome. Asmodeus alone was not elegantly dressed but wore the same black suit we knew from previous occasions. He asked Mother to leave the household chores to him. Again he extended the folding table and slid back the wall behind which another space allowed for encounters with the marvelous. Father and the Maestro had spent the day traveling to various oases in the desert in search of an appropriate spot to hold the party promised within the next few days. Helena had taken care of some correspondence in preparation for this affair the Maestro was hosting, and had remained in that reclusion so dear to the ladies, who can then sally forth from it clad in splendor and covered with gleaming stars. The little ones, Gaspar, Judith and Salome, had gone back to the Sarabias to pay their respects but had decided to switch their lodgings to the guest hostel where Helena and Asmodeus were staying. The change, it seemed, was more comfortable for all concerned.

Before sitting down to table we drank a delicious aperitif, provided by Asmodeus, that put us in a state of overflowing merriment. One by one various guests kept arriving from the village and, as at our previous dinner, the drink seemed to loosen everyone's tongue and good humor. Seated next to me, Helena told me a slave of hers had reported that he had been wandering in the desert and had caught me with one of his whips. The password—remember it the next time—is "beloveds." It will allow you to get through all obstacles until you reach the edge of my bed. She made a gracious gesture and reminded me I had nothing to worry about. What's more, she said, nodding toward Gaspar, Judith and Salome, those little ones are clowns for our entertainment and the fact is, whatever you want they have to do. I thanked her for her friendly counsel, perhaps in too quiet a voice. She put her bejeweled hand over my heart, shook her head and told me, You are easily depressed, like all poets. Drink to happiness! To illusions!

The entire party took their seats at the table, which lengthened whenever someone new arrived. Where there is bread for eight a ninth can always be invited, an old maxim of Mother's that was in operation today but multiplied fourfold: the Sarabias, Kruger, Siglic and his wife, the always tight-lipped and discreet Rossos, Irene Díaz and her effeminate husband, Gaona with his wife and children, my teacher Zoila Campana, Señor and Señora Durand, the Garzóns and their children. Now I felt I could recognize the faces and the characteristics that made each of them unique from all eternity.

Asmodeus, directing his team of invisible servants, kept us supplied with drinks and good things to eat; Gaspar and Salome ran from place to place making jokes and were the wonder of our neighbors, who gazed at them with a certain trepidation. The virtuous Inés, for her part, looked proud of every scoundrelly prank her children thought up. They had been within her womb, they had drunk—if rather reluctantly—her milk, and there they were, shining in beauty and genius.

Yes, what else could it be but a miracle! Last to arrive was Gustavo Schutt with Sara the mulatto. Sara's mother was sick and so they had been unable to arrive before the Maestro did, they said, apologizing profusely.

The gong sounded and we heard again the music coming from within the walls, transforming the once sober spirits of the diners into an ever more festive soirée. The Maestro was talking with Carlos and my sisters while Father recounted to me their great expedition along the entire coast of the Salar Grande, our great salt plain near which several oases occur. On the far side of the Salar there is a sprinkling of settlements that raise some crops and keep livestock. In each of these places Father had friends and they had been glad to see him.

Leaning close to my ear, he told me: We only had trouble in Socaire, where a religious fanatic followed us from the moment we entered the village and suddenly began to shout and accuse us of demonic intentions. We paid him no mind until he got ready to stone us, at which point Maestro Leonardo decided to teach him a lesson. There are millions of stones in that place and they all metamorphosed themselves into enormous flies the size of large rabbits and flew in and out and around every house and street in the town. That was no way to receive visitors, and so now the flies will keep them busy for days to come, said Father with a laugh. I saw in my mind's eye the tiny century-old hamlet with its adobe houses, its yards and trees, entirely covered by huge flies, and a shudder ran through me. It's cold up there, said Father, reading my thoughts, and it's always a welcome pleasure to get back home. I used to accompany him on mule back through those places, thinking to myself how the light off the salt flats can blind a man, how that cold thrusts weariness into the bones. Father was beaming, happy and content, enjoying a chat with Señorita Campana, whose new dress made her look very beautiful.

Helena, at my other side, touched my arm, producing in me the feeling of an electric shock. But Ludwig, she said laughingly, I barely touch you and you jump out of your seat. How are you going to escort me to the Maestro's party when it comes up in a few days? I too, she went on, am a woman of flesh and blood and I want to love you like one when the moment arrives. I felt her fingertips glide along my neck, and the impulse to clutch her to my breast was almost impossible to resist. Helena, Helena, I whispered.

Meanwhile my mother was telling the Maestro about the strange present delivered that afternoon. Leonardo laughed as at a good joke:

Bring the egg here, maybe we can decipher the meaning of this gift. My sisters ran to the closet and brought the box with its postcards and its treasure. What a great, great idea, admired our guest: if we boil this egg, the ostrich will come walking out. At that, Ida and Katty ran and came back with a portable stove and a large washbasin filled with water, in which they placed the egg. Helena proposed that we write names on it— the only way to control these beasts, because, she said, I see three of them through the shell-wall. We had to hurry: I suggested Olleb, Roderroc, and Osuli, since they're easy to remember. With her nails she inscribed on the speckled rind Bello, Corredor, and Iluso. Since they'll be seeing them from inside, she explained, they'll read them in reverse and answer only to these names.

The suspense mounted second by second. As the water began to boil, the shell of the huge egg started cracking and then broke; into our midst stepped three rheas which grew before our eyes as they walked along the table. When they had reached the height of a horse, the Maestro directed us to give them the water left in the basin: Let them drink it, otherwise they won't stop growing. We all laughed to see the immense birds act as though they were trained.

I got to my feet and called on everyone to toast the marvelous friend who had bestowed such a gift. They lifted their glasses and all cried in unison: To the poet Molina! To Enrique the Uncertain!

Now toasts for one thing and another went on repeating and intensifying, and the delicious foods brought by Asmodeus' invisible troop of servants were devoured ravenously, since it had been a long day and no one invited to this banquet had wanted to partake earlier of any of the usual insipid daily fare.

About two more hours had passed when Father invited all the guests to a special function that represented, he reminded them, the most ancient tradition of our ancestors. This was a trip to consult Sofia the medium about our forgotten dead. Everyone accepted and raised their glasses again, this time toasting Sofia, who for ever and ever had been the bridge between the invisible and the ordinary run of days.

The crystal bell rang once more and we all started across a twilight landscape toward the river meadows, where the long adobe wall stretches out. Gaspar, Judith and Salome did not resist the urge to mount the gigantic rheas, which raced each other and carried them hither and yon. The whole remainder of the village walked along slowly with us, our guests still enjoying the delights of the meal. And there in the distance we could make out a pair of tiny lights, maybe candles, toward which we were walking.

Sofia the Medium

As we walked I was watching my brother Carlos a few meters ahead of us, carrying his bag. What would come of this expedition we did not know, but it intrigued us. Drawing nearer we noticed, as we had that morning, the red-painted stakes driven into the earth, with ribbons of the same red tied to their tips like streamers. There was now a large crowd in the place, through which Father and the Maestro opened a way, allowing our group to draw nearest to the circle of colored sand within the stakes. At its center, with her long braids unbound, sat Sofia, who lived alone in a small hut by the river. More than serene, she seemed absent and took no notice of our arrival.

She was concentrating, like someone listening to the wind's voice, which speaks to seers about things that others can scarcely perceive. There in her circle Sofia began twisting her body and uttering guttural words; her muscles relaxed; now she might be an immense flower or a quiet animal that does not exist on this side of the veil.

Then a tiny, frail old woman with a falsetto voice pushed forward a holder with a lit candle until it touched the circle. This was Elvira Ossorio's mother, calling on her dead husband, Don Julián, to tell him his daughter was getting married and ask what he foresaw for her from the shadows. A few instants went by, though they seemed long to us, while the medium went through contortions on the ground. Suddenly she lifted her torso on her left arm and from her lips burst a man's voice seeming to come from far off.

"What do you want, you evil witch? Why are you blocking my

road with flames?" asked the voice of Don Julián. "It's because Elvira is getting married," said the old woman, terrified. "I think he's a good man, you knew him when he was a child, Sixto Lora. Remember?"

Another silence. The candle winked. Then all at once the medium, turning her head entirely around so that it faced backwards on her body, screamed: "Whores! Whores as you are! Why are you questioning me when you know your answer? I see Elvira crossing a canyon, her dress stained with red liquor; she seems to want to put the pieces of a pitcher back together but she can not. Filthy women, that's what you are! Unblock my road!" We saw the medium's convulsions redouble. With a certain shame Elvira's mother pulled her candle back from the circle.

Then I saw Humberto Gaona draw near, walking on his knees, to light a candle and touch it to the circle. It turned out that he was asking his dead godmother about the destiny of every person in his family. Again the medium was convulsed and again she fell still. In the darkness of night a woman's voice sounded, her tone serious, even solemn:

"I am listening. I smell a miasma rising from your house. Your sins will be purged by fire, but the fire will disperse you forever. Your wife's leprosy will spread and no one will want to look upon her face till the end of time. Your daughter will follow her mother's road. I see your oldest son standing before high walls, multitudes are shooting at him, he is being executed. Climb out of this well, Humberto, pray to the one who wears a red feather in his hat to have mercy, mercy on you!"

Humberto Gaona, pale as wax, moved his candle holder back from the circle. He seemed as though a huge dark stone had suddenly fallen and buried him, and everyone else there also came under the effect of his anguish.

Then the medium was speaking in the mocking voice of a man. "I am Necochea, my friends. The plague carried me off twenty years ago and no one remembers me. When I see your candles I think someone must be weeping for me, but it's useless, the horror of the plague has erased my memory in you. Say one thing for me: Cheers! I don't want prayers." I heard nervous laughter, coughing, then a murmur rising through the crowd: Cheers! Cheers, Necochea! I noticed that not a few of our companions were carrying some form or other of firewater under their ponchos: to drink to the dead.

I looked now at Carlos, wondering whether or not he would dare to present the head we had found that morning. My glance seemed to decide him. He took out a plate, put the head on it, and pushed this together with a lit candle into the circle. We saw the medium whirl around for a while and finally begin to speak in Quechua, but then fall silent and rigid. Beside me, the Maestro touched the skull with his walking stick and it suddenly covered itself with skin and with hair dressed in a complex knot. On its plate the head now seemed as though recently severed from its body. Its eyes wide open, with a long lamentation it began to speak, and immediately I heard the armadillo, perched on my shoulder, translate aloud for us what the dead girl was saying in her Indian language: "What do you want from me, brothers and sisters? My head was cut from my body and hidden in an oven. My name is Ata Ata and for hundreds of years I have been listening to the waters flow downstream. I never knew man's love and an incurable illness took me from you, lifting me toward the sun. What do you want, what troubles your hearts, my little sisters and brothers?"

One of the Puca brothers drew near and, also speaking in Quechua, said to the skull: "Curiosity made us conjure you, by your head we can tell how beautiful you were, perhaps I'm the man who would have been your spouse."

Again we heard the long lamentation and the head, moving its eyes, repeated a "Perhaps" that rang out like the tolling of a bell. Puca was struck dumb but he alone found the presence of mind to draw back the tiny light, dragging the candle out of the circle. At that instant the living head lost all its flesh and we saw only white bone shining in the moonlight.

Now Durand, intoning a spell, took Sofia's hand, trying to draw her out of the circle. But even the united strength of several men was not enough, until the Maestro touched the colored sand with his stick, making an opening through which we were finally able to bring the medium back from the power of the Spirits.

We were all overwhelmed, and relieved. Leonardo went over to Carlos and said: "It's not right to steal the work of the people below. Such mischief will be attempted in the future by others, condemned to arrogant madness about a pure race. Your transgression has saddened the heart of all these people." With his long fingers he touched Sofia's lips and she visibly regained color and animation, becoming again the person we knew in daily life.

Asmodeus rose as if from nowhere and in the Zapotec manner poured a tiny glass of liquor and drank it off in one swallow. Then he was offering each person in the crowd a drink of this liquid as red as blood that would "put the souls back in our bodies and the joy in our minds." I saw the Maestro link arms with my parents and I did the same with Helena for the slow walk back.

Happiness now seemed to have returned and drenched all our hearts. My father, a couple of steps ahead of me, said to Maestro Leonardo with a certain tinge of nostalgia: "Do you remember the heat in Batavia? Here it's not much different, cold at dawn, but there's never that bewitchment of snowfall, those petals covering everything in white." "Your desires haven't changed, Guillermo my friend," responded our courtly guest. "Twenty-four hours won't pass before we see that white miracle you long for so much."

Helena, on my arm, was asking me about my childhood and smiling at the answers. Always demanding the impossible, she said. Nobody wants to hear the truth, they all just want to be loved. That's a rather overused aphorism, she went on. I prefer the one you invented in dispraise of the camel. I laughed, but she added in a solemn tone: "Winding the Impossible" is an image in which I see you next to a woman-doll pictured from the waist up, her palm touching the palm of another woman seen against the sky. A small lizard contemplates the scene. It's a painting by Susana, and though someone will steal it using evil arts, the affair will bring good luck. Remind me when it happens! I promised to give her all the details if this event should occur. It seemed impossible to me at that moment that I would ever forget her least gesture.

As on the previous nights, this stroll under the ivory moon was a true gift for everyone who had been invited to enjoy the evening's party. On the horizon at times we noticed a flickering over the volcanoes: the distant storm that gives birth to the waters of our river. Walking arm in arm with the lovely Helena Ferrucchi seemed a dream, but through her slender fingers I felt the torrents plunge, driven by the turbine of the heart. Then yes, it would be possible for me to make a poem, the poem, any poem I would please—the stars had assigned my destiny.

The Strange History of Helena Ferrucchi

lthough Helena was walking arm in arm with me, although her hip was touching my side, I felt suddenly that she was far away, absent. I turned and caught a glint of sadness in her eyes, which seemed to be looking across an invisible landscape. Taking her by the shoulders, I held her to my chest and kissed her tear-moist eyelids. Whatever's troubling you, I said, tell me; pain's always lessened if you can share it...even if it's only with me. She made a gesture as if to say, don't talk foolishness!

But she reacted and, as though returning from an old and sad remembrance, sobbed in my arms. After a time, she seemed to push her anguish aside and said: "It's so difficult, your loving me." She fell silent for a while and then, her fingers interwoven with mine, remembering, she began to speak.

"More than a century ago I lived in the house of my parents, who ruled with an iron hand over the southern part of Italy facing the Adriatic Sea. As a daughter of nobles, no whim of mine arose without everyone hurrying to indulge it. One morning some people told me that a few days earlier a ship had anchored by the group of rocks and small rocky islands along the coast. The owner's intention wasn't to fish or do business of any kind: they had seen him, a foreign painter who seemed enchanted with the place, leave his ship and go by boat to some of the barren islets where there were ancient ruins. Because my family's property extended offshore to these rocks and islands, I decided to take a pair of faithful servants and see what it was that attracted the foreign painter. One calm day I set sail and a gentle breeze carried our boat to a landing a little above the painter's anchorage. We went up the gang-plank of a small ship which might once have been a pilot boat but was outfitted and painted in an extraordinary style. Stepping on deck, I saw the artist with his back to me, so immersed in whatever he was doing that he did not notice our presence. When I was only a few steps from him, he turned without warning and looked at me, as frightened as if I were an apparition.

I introduced myself and told him that only curiosity had com-pelled me to come with my servants to see what subject attracted an artist to our parts. He smiled, and despite his graying reddish beard his face appeared to me like the face of a being glimpsed in dreams. He approached and, kissing my fingertips, said in an accent I recognized as German: Allow me to present myself. My name, though it will tell you little, is Arnold Böcklin. I've lived in Italy for a long time, but it's only recently, while painting these rocks, that it has seemed to me I have found the center of my world.

With each passing instant I felt closer in my heart to this stranger. The rocks, as he made me see them, resembled ruins or maybe tombs, and I remembered that all the fishermen and local inhabitants never set foot on them out of a belief that they brought bad luck. I told the artist this but he laughed and ordered two of his sailors to bring a bottle of red wine "to celebrate such lovely visitors." After hours that seemed to pass like seconds, I said good-bye to Arnold, promising to come see him in the next few days. He was staying at an inn in the nearby port and he promised to show me some sketches for his paintings. As my servants and I returned to our boat, I felt my heart throbbing like a frightened bird's.

But I couldn't wait a few days. I was awake most of the night thinking about the mysterious stranger.

The next morning, taking advantage of the fact that my mother was away on a trip to Palermo, I decided to go see the painter in love with rocks. Although the wind blew favorably, our boat made slow progress and the delay seemed to me unbearably long. When I went up the white gangplank of the anchored ship, I saw that Arnold was wait-ing for me. As soon as we had greeted each other, he said: I didn't sleep at all last night, I've thought a great deal about you, Helena, and if you're willing, I want to take you to visit the island ruins that have subjugated me as if they were part of some enchantment.

Lightly, I said that in a small boat and with a fairly strong oarsman we could probably explore all the abandoned islands: the rocks were, as chance would have it, part of my family's property and there was no problem in our leaving the boat and investigating them. Arnold was perhaps fifty years old and his hair and beard were beginning to turn gray, but something in him was supremely attractive to me and so I deliberately put aside all the usual formalities and we sailed that same afternoon with Homer, a family servant who knew the intricate coastal channels well. Moment by moment the high ramparts grew closer and clearer: in their center arose a dense stand of dark green cypresses, and the forms of the ruined buildings suggested that there were galleries and secret rooms inside the rocks.

We approached a kind of terrace that once might have served as a landing. Arnold jumped to the ground and held out his hand to me. We asked Homer to watch the boat so that it would not strike against the rocks and set out to explore the island. I never imagined that this action would mark my destiny forever."

Helena was silent for a moment while we walked in the desert; then, turning toward me, she continued. "Arnold and I explored all over the small island, which in ancient times had probably been used by some cult. Among the rocks we discovered galleries and rooms, but we couldn't see them well because they were dark and we hadn't thought to bring oil lamps along.

Maybe the strangeness of the place, or my extreme youth, made possible the passion that was now growing up like tropical vegetation, drawing and binding us together. Everything but kissing and embracing—as though we were going to devour each other—seemed to us useless, senseless. However, Arnold was a very gentlemanly person and maintained toward me, despite his passion, a certain reserve.

We saw each other almost every day for two weeks. When my mother returned I invited him to come to our ancestral home, which for all its provincialism contained many paintings and antique curiosities. Mother too seemed enchanted with the artist; a widow and youthful still, she told me one day that it was she perhaps who could better understand the painter. From that point the two of us maintained silence about him but sordid jealousy poisoned our relationship forever.

On Arnold's visits to the house he brought a series of paintings that fascinated both of us. His canvases and drawings included many depictions of the abandoned islands, as well as nudes and portraits. Among these were two or three self-portraits showing the painter next to a being without flesh, a skeleton dressed in black that played the violin and functioned as a distorted mirror image of the vitality and beauty the artist's own face reflected. With the imprudence of youth I asked him several times about this person, his companion in his self-portraits, and each time he gave a vague answer that didn't satisfy but only increased my curiosity. Now, too, the conflict between me and my mother, the jealousy we felt, rose to an icy peak when we discovered to our surprise that the painter was having passionate relations with both of us. We were not mother and daughter but two women fighting over a man they both loved.

My mother in her desire and fury wanted to put me into a convent in Palermo where my aunt was abbess. Anguished at what I felt was a betrayal, I demanded Arnold to reveal who was his choice. He replied anxiously that he was a victim of strange powers he could not reveal to me. He was not able, he said, to do anything but obey his interior being. I intuitively felt that he was referring to the fleshless specter that appeared over and over again in his paintings. I refused to hear any more and went that summer to Palermo, where my aunt welcomed me.

Months had passed and winter was approaching when my aunt spoke to me, happy that it seemed she had saved my soul and my life. You arrived here, little one, in such a state that I believed each day might be your last. In your fever you cried out the name Arnold, who, I now know, is the famous painter who lives near Rome. Your mother fell deeply in love with him...she died last month, of a fever, they say. I didn't want to tell you before, because your health was so delicate and fragile. But you are the only heir; you must go now and claim your family inheritance.

The news left me mute. Where was Arnold?

My aunt went on: I have also received a letter for you from Rome. If you feel strong enough...I hope it will bring you good news. She held out to me a thick envelope with my name and address. In one corner were the painter's initials in gold, and in manuscript letters: Strictly private.

Despite my weakness I seized the envelope, and my aunt said she would go so that I could read the letter calmly. In case you feel any discomfort, she advised me, I'm leaving you this bell. If it rings, I'll return immediately to help you; in the meantime I will be in the park praying for you.

The note, on a parchment with drawings, contained the following words in large, clear script:

"To the Contessa Helena Ferrucchi:

I hope that the air of Palermo has been beneficial to your health. From your aunt, the abbess of the convent of the Sisters of Saint Joseph, you may have learned the sad news about your mother. If this is so, I pray that you pardon me and not try to see me, because I don't wish to burden my soul with any more nightmares.

Many times you asked me about the figure included in my self-portraits; now I can tell you, it is Maestro Leonardo—some would call him the devil—whom I promised I would paint as my companion if I achieved fame. My show in Rome has fascinated the entire world, to the extent that two or three of the paintings of your deserted islands are being fought over by a score of rich men.

Helena, maybe I am not the man destined for you. Speak, if you ever have a chance, with Leonardo, the Maestro. He has assured me that in 1927, 100 years after me, a poet will be born in the desert on the other side of the world. If you are willing to serve as the Maestro's secretary for this long trial, almost a century, you will find a man and you will be loved and sung by him.

Forgive me and do not try to see me.

Arnold Böcklin."

I took to my bed anew, consumed by fever. In my dreams Maestro Leonardo called me many times. I know that you are not laying a trap with him but only trying to put a little humanity into his millennia-old Face. I don't know if I am a living being or only a spirit, I've traveled through hundreds of countries and mingled with all the races on the planet. When I saw you in the train, your image recalled the one I had loved madly, you resemble him so much. I was afraid for myself and for you, that's why I trembled to lift the veils of illusion from your eyes. Ludwig, Ludwig. Will you be able to love me, now that you know my unhappy history?"

I heard her sigh on my arm, and a tenderness toward that fragile being united with the passion I had felt for her from the first. Helena, I said, I have eaten your tongue. It's given me the marvelous flavor of your soul, and kindled a passion I wouldn't know how to put out.

We had arrived at my house. The moonlight shone on Helena's naked shoulders. Rest here, on my bed, I said, I'll stay with you until day returns. I saw her fall asleep in my arms, a strange rush of waves broke on the rocks in the paintings of Böcklin. Birds were making nests in dark cypresses stirring in the ocean breeze.

It was very late before, wrapped in alpaca covers at the foot of the bed where Helena was sleeping, I was finally able to doze off.

The day just ended had left me with such sharp sensations that sleep came at first as a friend and restorer. I had been asleep maybe two or three hours when from the depths of me there emerged a strange dream.

"The first image that rises before my sight: there, look! Leviathan! And it seemed that I must fight this sea serpent many times larger than my size. I see myself as a part of ancient woodcuts that depict it: I am holding a sword, my only possibility of salvation. The important thing is to split the serpent horizontally, that is, along its entire length, and this is what I do, not knowing from where I draw the strength. The interior of the reptile is black and recalls the asphalt and tar used on roads, but I don't know why. I see that the serpent has shrunk and that I can lift it into the air and carry it on my back. If I can hold it up I can control it; it will renew its life and size if I let it submerge itself in the water.

Next I decide to spread the pieces of the serpent out flat. I arrange them and, using some of the liquid asphalt innards, paste them on the rocks and somehow construct a road that grows to gigantic, monolithic proportions, running along the left side of a mountain. I repeat to myself: I have brought the serpent this far, with the intention of reaching the lost paradise—which is how I envision the country formed by these high mountains that enring a blue lake, its shores covered with tender greenery that sends a feeling of happiness through the surrounding countryside.

I shout across the water of the lake. I appear to live there, for I see amid the vegetation a large, isolated house. At my cry, from the bottom of the lake emerges an incandescent globe that transforms into a solid, crystallized world spinning in space. I do not understand the meaning of this, since the lake is not a volcano and the phenomenon is produced simply by shouting over the water, precisely at the border between the two worlds.

I go down then into the interior of the water to see what causes this occurrence. The country there is covered in beauty, and I see a species of living caryatids who support an immense underwater building from which the globes of fire rise. Each time someone shouts at the edge of the water, these lover-mothers feel a pressure within them that obliges them to set loose a portion of the subterranean magma, which solidifies and crystallizes in the air, becoming a new world.

It is the power of the word, I tell myself, it is the possibility of the creative that produces this phenomenon; be alert to the things of the unconscious, or the unconscious will remain submerged in the water. The caryatids in the dream are in very dynamic poses, like erotic sculptures in the temples of India; they have none of the stateliness that would recall classical Greek figures."

A Singular Day

We were awakened by someone pounding on the bedroom door. It was my father, drunk with enthusiasm, calling to us: Children, get up! Come see this marvel!

We put on jackets and I went out with Helena, who also had been awakened by Father's shouts of joy. From the porch we saw what was causing the commotion. Everything, for as far as the eye could see, was covered with twenty centimeters of snow. My father ran around like a child from house to house waking up everyone in the village. Here's the snow! Here's the snow!

We saw the Maestro, the Sarabias, and all the people Father's cries had roused coming toward our house. My brother and sisters and I, who had never seen such a spectacle, were already making snowballs. Father hugged the Maestro, who smilingly reminded him that he had foretold this snowfall the previous night.

A sort of madness seemed to inhabit the frozen whiteness. Father said to everyone: It's nearly dawn. Let's make a snowman! So children and adults armed with shovels piled up snow in front of our house. In half an hour we had shaped it all into a figure three meters high with a scarf around its neck, two apples for eyes, and a carrot for a nose. Someone ran off in search of a straw hat to crown the work; the completed snowman made us all laugh.

Father did not have a good voice, but neighbors sang songs as if this were a sort of carnival. The sun began to rise over the hills and, just as it had been surprising to see the snowflakes, it was incredible to see them melt away into the sand. An hour later only the scarf, the apples and the worn-out hat marked the place where the snowman had been.

Asmodeus, ever attentive, had brought out hot chocolate and rolls, which we drank and devoured with a joy we had never felt before and perhaps would never repeat.

We saw our friend Gustavo Schutt coming at a run from the other side of the village. My father shouted that he had missed seeing the most splendid snow figure in the desert. But seemingly our neighbor had other worries. He told us agitatedly that his mother-in-law, Doña Tomasa, had just died. All night she had been in a delirium, and at various times had made her daughter and Gustavo promise by the most sacred thing they believed in to carry her for her funeral to the church on the square in nearby Calama. The sick old woman was afraid that the wake might take place in Río Loa, which would mean asking for the big table from the kitchen in our house, on which the dead were always laid out—it was the only sufficiently large table in the village. In her delirium she told them it was a table for the damned, because often, when she had gone to say good-bye to some departed person, it seemed to her the table was burning. It filled her with evil forebodings.

Gustavo had promised to fulfil the pledge that, in the circumstances, they had made to her. He had come to inform us he would be gone for the day, seeking a casket to carry the body of the old woman to Calama and arranging with the Calama priest, who had a reputation as a madman, to permit the laying out in his church of a stranger to his flock, one who had never, as far as anyone could verify, so much as gone to confession. Gustavo Schutt's story dissipated the last sparks of enchantment that the snow had produced in us, but the fact that it was his mother-in-law and not his adored Sara who had passed to the other world seemed to have settled him.

Gustavo's news and the vanishing of the last traces of the snowflakes dispersed all the people who had gathered. It was mid-morning and we invited the Maestro and Helena to join us for breakfast on the porch. Asmodeus called the little ones, Gaspar, Judith and Salome, who arrived quickly mounted on the enormous ostriches that they seemed to have adopted as the means of ideal transport, flitting from place to place in the village.

The day had begun strangely. Now Father said good-bye because he had things to do at the dynamite factory, and my mother and sisters and brother were left to look after our visitors. We seated them in Chinese wicker armchairs for coffee with biscuits and especially for a chance to exchange impressions of what we had seen. The Maestro was smiling complacently and tried to answer the questions that we put to him, who had traveled through dozens of countries in remote times and looked fearlessly on the strangest events. When he saw Helena's fingers and mine interlaced he laughed suggestively, saying to me: I see you've found the woman of your dreams. My only regret is losing an assistant for whom I've developed a sincere regard. Maybe we won't have only one wedding tonight, since I see that the phantasms of the painter have disappeared from the eyes of our beloved contessa, and it looks like the terms have been met. I saw Helena gaze at him pleadingly. Yes, said the Maestro, I've known it from all eternity: 1827, 1927. People today seem to have forgotten the portrait Arnold did of me. To me he said: I hope that you, having conquered the fears and terrors of childhood, can write some accounts of my life. Your secretary will never abandon you, he said with a glance at Helena. And you work with the best translator one could imagine. I prefer not to mention the ivory book, because one never knows when reckless, insane jealousies can be stirred up, and this is something that neither you nor your father has ever been able to learn. He laughed aloud. It's nothing to get solemn about. Asmodeus, bring that Italian wine you've been saving all these years. Now's the time to toast lovers who will love for all eternity. The glasses were filled and everyone wished long life to mad love, which here and now, between Helena and me, was real. When we finished our drinks I noticed that the wind, which had been blowing softly for the last few hours, had grown unquiet: only a short time now and the mirages would begin to strike the railings of our porch in their continuous metamorphoses.

The mirages are a dream that is realized on the physical plane; they have an interpretation, but they can also be interpreted as a dream, since they correspond to another face of our reality. I believed I was thinking these things to myself but found that Leonardo was reading my thoughts. It's true, he answered me, but this idea takes you toward the skepticism that all is illusion, one reality continuously mixing with another.

Then let me tell you, I said, what I am seeing, here, right in front of us.

"The images spread until they disappear.
I am in a Near Eastern country, maybe Libya, maybe Israel. There are many likenesses between the landscapes and settlements of these

countries and those of northern Chile. The buildings are of mud and cane, a form of construction that I saw when I was a child, but all is in disorder, the people are running away and it's hard for me to tell what is going on, why they are afraid, why they do not want to talk to me when I approach them.

The crowd passes through an intricate network of streets and finally I perceive that I may be in a park that ends in a beautiful art nouveau building. But now all is in a state of warfare and destruction. I resolve to determine what is happening. I have on strong mountain-climbing shoes, and I climb the canes and bricks till I reach the third floor, where I see seated, next to a wall, a young woman, a venerable old man and a little boy. I stand in front of them and ask them to explain why the crowd flees at my approach.

The old man answers me: Don't you see that at every moment you are accompanied by an invisible woman? I look next to me. If what he says is true, she must indeed be invisible, since I can make out no presence. They repeat that they see her, that she is very beautiful and wise, a type of angel that protects but at the same time inspires fear in many. I wake up with the sense of a revelation, a miracle of which I am part."

That's what I've been telling you, Leonardo said. And now you have the advantage of being able to see that woman with your eyes. Looking at Helena, he went on: The men in your mirage have a species of premonitory dream, she is "very beautiful and wise." If somehow you don't see it, nevertheless it's engraved in your heart.

The heat had turned suffocating and mirages were following one another in quick succession. Long blue beaches, where ships or unknown plants and animals pass by. A butterfly seems suddenly to be within reach, but one approaches a meter closer and it is moving away, changing into a steamy vapor over which images flicker.

From the house to the left of ours, Señorita Zoila Campana now came walking toward us. Her dress of flowered veils extended almost to the ground. As always when she went out, she was wearing a large hat and also carrying a parasol that some friend must have brought her from the ports of China, or so our fantasy proposed.

Her every movement had that refinement which the coarse attribute to affectation. Arriving at our porch, she greeted all of us with a smile and asked pardon for interrupting. We rose to greet her and offered her some of the coffee liqueur on the table, and a chair in which she could feel comfortable and at ease. She was a delicate and fragile woman and, perhaps due to her education, excessively timid. It was a rare occasion when she left her house for any other reason than to walk to the little school. She never visited anyone and it was strange that she had determined to cross the garden between the two houses and speak to us so directly.

We attributed the event to that peak of curiosity that occurs customarily in all woman, but maybe we were wrong. While she was taking little sips of her liqueur, she told us that she had had a dream that night and on account of it wanted to speak with Maestro Leonardo. We made as if to leave so that she could talk about it privately, but with a decisiveness we had not imagined in her, she said: I have nothing to hide and it's better that you all hear it from my mouth than from the whispers on the wind.

She breathed deeply, as if to take heart, and turning to the Maestro, she began: "Everyone in this village knows that I come from a very traditional, religious family, in which for generations some of the daughters took vows as nuns in cloistered convents. My parents thought, given my character, it was possible that I was chosen for this religious life. I tried to follow their good counsels, but each time I visited the bell tower next to the convent I suffered a fainting spell that would last for minutes or even extend into a coma-like stupor that kept me in bed for days. That was why I had to renounce the plan of professing my vows as a religious, and I dedicated myself instead to teaching.

Once I had a dream. I was hidden, it seemed, in a subterranean cell and my body was covered with welts from the lashes I suffered—perhaps voluntarily, perhaps not—at the hands of a small dwarf with a malignant face who cracked his whip over my bleeding back. Exhausted finally, and annoyed by I know not what, he took a metal belt heated red-hot over a brasier and said to me: Know that as long as this belt of nails is fastened around you, no man will approach you and you will not be able to love, not even someone you desire. He applied the instrument of torture to my body and such was the pain that I lost consciousness.

When I woke the next day, fever and anguish devoured me, and although it had been a dream, I felt condemned. Within two days my parents' care and love had set me on the path to recovery, but still on my waist there was a chain of wounds, burns impressed in the flesh by a belt studded with nails. Over the years this has tormented me. I can't remove it from my body, and the burns are renewed, causing me to recoil, each time there appears some man who could love me. Even when the children show me their innocent affection, fear of involving them in my suffering makes me draw back." She stopped due to the force of her emotion and the evident effort it cost her to tell these sad things. She sipped a little water, then continued: "I believed this was my road, mapped out by fate. Only in the last two days, since I saw the Zellers' son arrive, now a man and accompanied by such distinguished visitors, have I felt that my life might take some other course. The night before last, as we walked past your house, among the flowers I found a card I thought I had seen in the Maestro's hands earlier in the evening. I took it and kept it to look at again later.

Last night, in the darkness, I remembered the old card and was moved to examine it more carefully. I didn't turn on the light: the card was shining more brightly than a candelabrum and entirely illuminating its own face. It was made of a thick parchment stamped with ancient engravings. But looking more closely, I saw with surprise that the engraved figures were moving as if to open a path to some person who was arriving. The true surprise was that I myself was the person I saw in the card, looking back at me and laughing as she said: Stop torturing yourself uselessly. Then she began to take off her clothes, which she cast to the winds until she stood completely naked. She, that is, I, went then to the venerable Maestro, who was there in the card, and he dipped a brush in wine, chanting: 'Let it be blotted out, let it be blotted out, let the wind take it so that it never returns.' He painted brushstroke after brushstroke of red wine on my wounds and little by little they began to disappear. When not even the smallest sign remained of the hairshirt that had tortured me for years, the Maestro gave me a cup of the same wine and said: Everything must happen as in your dreams; after you have drunk this wine, the equivalent of blood, kiss the first man that you know could have loved you and you will be cured forever.

I woke some hours ago and saw the snow falling on the sand, which seemed a miracle. Couldn't something similar happen to me? I've been worrying over this for hours. I saw the Maestro on your porch and decided to follow the dictates of my heart." She stopped, as if ashamed to have spoken of something prohibited; I saw her close her eyes and wait to see what reaction her words had caused.

We kept silent while the Maestro, the one she truly had come to consult, withheld any reply. We heard him pronounce two sentences in Aramaic to Helena Ferrucchi before finally turning to our teacher and saying: Thanks, dear friend, for the confidence you've shown us in telling us such sad events. I don't want to repeat the dream here in the open air, in front of everyone, so I'm asking Helena to take you into this hospitable house. My mother agreed readily. We, the Maestro added, will wait for you to make the toast with the wine of blood.

We watched Señorita Zoila follow Helena to my parents' bedroom. Asmodeus brought a black ceramic jar and a palette with a paintbrush that Leonardo asked mother to take to Helena. It is you, Señora Rosa, with your goodwill, who can best help Zoila: please stay with them, said Asmodeus. To each of us—Carlos, Katty, Ida, Kuni and me—he gave a card: This way you will be able to watch the magical cure and transformation of Señorita Zoila, he told us.

Truly, as if it were a looking glass, each card showed what was happening on the other side of the wall. To encourage Zoila, Helena touched her thin lips with the paintbrush of wine. What we saw was almost impossible for our eyes to accept: Zoila Campana tore her dress of veils to pieces, the delicate bits of cloth fell to the ground in tatters and in an instant we saw a white and graceful body emerge, its only distinguishing mark a blood-colored zone around the waist. Helena dipped the brush in wine again and passing it over this belt she pronounced the prayer: "Let it be blotted out, let it be blotted out, let the wind take it so that it never returns."

Then she repeated it in the language we supposed to be Aramaic and we saw the wounds, like a torturer's belt, disappearing from the marvelous body before our eyes. When every sign of them was gone, Helena emptied the rest of the wine of blood into the shallow ceramic dish and offered it to Zoila. She drank it down and it seemed to fill her with a prodigious energy: she wrapped herself in a semitransparent robe my mother was holding and came out, full of happiness, to see us on the porch. Her eyes burned with inspiration at what had happened. She looked around at us all and then, her eyes piercing into mine, said: I saw you so many times, as a boy, devour me with a look, I can't give anyone else the first kiss I give as a woman to a man. I am sure of the reality of your love. She came to me and I felt her lips burning mine like coals while her arms clutched me.

Everyone was cheering, and I, a little abashed, tried to laugh. Helena took me by the hand and giving me another kiss, she said, I hope that this way you can get over your childhood amours.

Asmodeus brought glasses and we all toasted love.

Zoila Campana, with a spirit we had never known her to possess, hugged the Maestro and ran across the garden to her house. She was the image of happiness, she did not wear a hat or carry a sunshade, and for the first time she seemed to enjoy the desert sun.

Stringing Dreams Together

y now it was hours past noon and the Maestro said apologetically that he had to leave: Business awaits, we'll see each other tonight. We saw him hail a car and set off with Gaspar, Salome and Judith on the road toward the San Pedro volcano, beyond the barren region of the Salar.

My mother and my brother and sisters went to arrange things for the wedding to be celebrated that night and left Helena and me to take care of the house. Sitting on the porch, we watched the wind rising, the wind that disperses the last mirages. Vortices of warm air appeared from time to time and moved like great columns in the desert. I remembered how as a child I had made enormous cardboard wheels and set them rolling over the sand. The wind would carry them far away and three days later, or ten, we'd often see them return. The real problem was to run and stop them. Always we had written on them poems or prayers to someone far beyond our sight, and we hoped that one day an answer would come back.

Seeing me contemplating the whirlwinds, Helena smiled. Those are children's games, she said, and to her lips came a tone as of a singer singing mockery in Italian. She was delighted with the childhood extravagances I told her about. I, on the other hand, seem to have lived an endless dream, she said, in which thousands of beings disintegrate, one after another, into dust. And maybe in those dreams I've been cruel, even malevolent. Every being has a shadow place in its heart. Her face darkened and that melancholy look I had noticed before appeared in her eyes.

If we all have a secret, dark place in our being, I said, then I have one too. And now that your hand's in mine I can tell you that I haven't achieved holiness, only a thirst for the absolute, which I've tried to find in many women.

Helena sensed I was about to tell her some episode from my life and facing me she said: If only you realized I know the thirst that devours you better than you do! I see it each time I lose myself in the depths of your eyes. It's something I've waited years for, and now I know it by heart...I am it, made visible to you. I saw her smile and I felt shame. Did she know more about me than I did myself?

She took me in her arms: You'll never again have to wait for the woman dreamed. I'm here because of a destiny written centuries ago, and the only thing I have not already seen is your dreams, which play out in a parallel universe. If you want to give me the gift that would be most precious to me, tell me your dreams. Then I'll know the other roads and faces you've confronted over the long years. Don't be afraid, she repeated; whatever life is, to the end of eternity I'll be beside you taking the forms of your desire. She seemed to me so warm and beautiful in her dress of radiant colors that I lay down at her side and put my head in her lap. Her face, her lips, were like an apparition. The sweetness of her touch drew me down into dream.

"It appears that Susana and I are on a trip or doing some sightseeing. We've arrived at a sort of hotel, very primitive, that reminds me of the pictures of buildings bombed during the war. The place is located in the upper part of Las Condes Avenue, somewhat beyond the Cultural Institute. The employees are pleasant, simple people, very backward.

We have only ordered a drink, being thirsty, but it appears that through some error they have registered us in the hotel. Susana is disgusted by this, but truly it is not important. On a paper fastened to the wall is the list of guests, among them L. Zeller, thus, without any other notation. What can one expect, I try to explain to Susana, everyone here is so primitive, all with that typical air of the middle-class Chilean, gray-black clothes and little neatly trimmed mustaches in the style of Homero Arce.

We walk around the poorly furnished old house; there is almost no light and the floors are of packed earth. Maybe magnificent marble flooring exists, but if so, no one is concerned to put it in order. The place must once have been a great mansion, I think, but now only the stone walls remain, the twisted iron railings and the dust. A few small trees, typical of old country houses, are the only living vegetation. Did a disaster occur at some point? Or has the house always been this way? I can't tell nor is there anyone to ask.

We find ourselves with Amparo and Eugenio Granell, the painter. They too are on a journey. We chat about something, I don't know what, something difficult to resolve. All of us are standing around a table trying to complete forms that our friends have to fill out. Then Susana and I approach a small stand on which curious paper cutouts are exhibited. At first one would have said they are Chinese but later we realize they are in a different style. It seems that we buy something.

Looking at the mud walls I see the name, perhaps the very signature, of the poet Rosamel del Valle written there. I point it out to the innkeeper, but he says it is now the signature of another man, who is standing right beside us: a person dressed in black, in a simple style just like that of Rosamel himself, watchful, as if desirous of being noticed. He asks me if I am staying at the hotel and I say yes.

We go out onto the patio. Maybe we would have liked to leave, to do something else. The place is falling down and there is a sorrowful sense of abandonment. Viewed from the garden, at a distance, it seems nothing but a ruin surrounded by bushes; nevertheless, we return resolutely to the house, since a film is going to start. Quite naturally I lie down with Susana in the bed in front of the screen, a little to the right of center. One very crude bench, five or six meters long, provided for those who might want to watch, remains empty. But I don't see anyone arrive, and there's no film, either. Under the blankets we look at each other and make love. We notice that the coverlets are torn, there has been no attempt to mend them, that everything here, as in the rest of the building, has been abandoned.

We get up. We will have to go eat, I suppose. Now on the bench are spread various cutouts in pale red paper, not unlike those that I myself make. We buy some and I put them in a book to preserve them from damage. Then we move toward the interior of the house, where there stands an old woman—Susana, maybe?—and a little girl four or five years old, who very seriously, as if following a ritual, shows me a small bluish-gray velvet bag, about fifteen by twenty centimeters, in which she is carrying a tiny boy child, very fragile, well-proportioned but with an immense head.

She speaks and tells me that the small boy is named Ludwig Zeller.

With great care I pick him up. He becomes slightly larger, and I try to control the head so that it is not injured. Strangely, the boy talks like a wise adult. The little girl had explained to me that it was difficult to make him eat because his mouth is so small; now, however, it is certainly he who is speaking to me. He asks what language I prefer. I tell him: Spanish, since that is the only language I understand.

He responds that it doesn't matter, he can translate from any language. It seems that he reads minds and can express the inexpressible. He talks to me as from another world or another plane. If only you knew, he tells me, how images are amplified (like a 'blow up' on photographic paper) to reveal all details, even the most minute.

I see that the being in my arms, with all his fragility, is an exceptional mentality capable of seeing objects and beings from the future or the past. And that my duty may be to care for him and make him grow. So many aspects of this being impress me as familiar that it seems right for him to bear my name; and it is necessary to prevent him from suffering the mischances I have met in this life.

Maybe he is my double, my angel, my other self."

I felt the sensation of waking up, of resting my head not on pillows but on the softest lap I would ever find. Helena passed her fingertips over my forehead and asked me: Why are you still suffering? I don't know, I told her, there's something in the past I don't understand. Sometimes it prevents me from going my way in peace; it's as if the whole world were in desolation. She placed her fingers on my eyelids again and in a very low voice said to me: Continue dreaming.

"I am visiting in my mother's house, which is built of wood beautifully maintained in its natural color. But inside there is not one picture, object or piece of furniture, nothing but walls, doors, windows. The floor is packed dirt, there are no floorboards. I wonder what has happened. My mother, who seems very contrite, tells me that Father is extremely weak. I go to what would be his bedroom and see him in a dressing gown, indeed terribly weak and thin.

He comes and embraces me; or rather, I have the feeling of someone falling into my arms. His head is thrown back and I realize that it is the body of Christ as sculpted by Michelangelo in the arms of the Virgin. Then I am outside, on an immense plain with bushes one and a half meters high in a dry riverbed. In the distance are mountains of an intense blue color. Maybe it's dawn or dusk, there is a moon.

I see a man on horseback galloping in my direction. The animal is black and reminds me of ancient Tibetan or Mongolian engravings. The rider's trappings and armament are also exotic. He approaches closer and closer and does not stop the animal when he is a few strides away but knocks me down and rides over me. It seems that in all this there is some danger, something indefinite that floats in the air. I return to my parents' house."

I felt Helena's fingertips caressing my temples, giving me strength in my moments of weakness. You must have patience, she says to me, the water will come eventually, from inside. I feel her lips touch my eyelids.

"I am in a large mansion two or three stories high, in the colonial style, with square patios; beyond them, looking across arcades and through windows, one sees many levels in which a community lives. The house is a Jesuit residence, and the time seems very late at night. I know in the dream that I have to leave a message, though I don't know either its content or form. The only thing clear to me, as I explore the corridors in semi-darkness, is that it will be difficult to find my way out again, and that from this place I can see 'other worlds.' I notice that strange beings and people, in formal dress, are dancing. A young man who walks beside me shows me how I can return to my room; I'm unable to make out his face, since everything is seen from above.

Then I am near a small square that once existed in Río Loa. The half moon rises across the zenith of the sky, producing a milky light. All at once I discover that it is not the moon but a new star shining there in the heights. It only looks somewhat like the half-moon, but it is more shapeless. My first thought is that it might be habitable for humans, but immediately I realize this is impossible. It is made of phosphorus, which is why it shines, but no vegetation or water exists there.

I walk in the square, now accompanied by Father and by others who approach, then recede into the desert. All of them are women who later disappear, being converted into small heaps of sand approximately fifty centimeters in diameter, similar in structure to those that clams leave on the beach. But no clams are seen, only the alternating hollows and sand heaps. I recognize one of the women, Denise Doré, illuminated by the phosphorescent light of the new star in the sky. It is pleasant to see her again, very beautiful, as in the best moment of her life.

Later Father and I go to an open tunnel. It is like a gash in the desert but I think 'tunnel' because I see there are sluice gates at intervals in it. We advance inside that gully-tunnel on a platform that slides along rapidly. On the wall, to the right, I see neon lights that flash and spin, also very rapidly, although a little ahead no further advance is possible because here magnets shut the floodgates. I understand that it is thanks to Father's knowledge and love that I've been able to enter this unknown desert place, from which somehow one can see and study other beings.

In a second part of the dream I walk through the suburbs of a city where I lived thirty years ago. The buildings are old, one to three stories high: businesses, homes, etc. I and another person move along the right side of the street, not on the sidewalk but within the buildings themselves. Like spirits we can pass through walls: there are passageways from house to house.

We arrive at a place where drinks are being served; on the patios I see trucks, and people working. But I realize that Yolanda lives there, which makes me uncomfortable, and I try not to run into her. I don't see her and discover that the resident is really a very beautiful woman who is seated, meditating, surrounded by giant crystal balls. The grouping, seen from a distance, forms an immense mandala of lights in an intense shade of blue. The meditating woman is timid and pure, like a child. I speak to her lovingly, but she signals me that her father, who is there with someone else, is watching her. The father and the person with him are dressed entirely in white, like Hindus, and are trying to decipher a book of mantras, written in an oriental language—Arabic or Hindi perhaps—and bound in white leather.

I realize that by looking into and listening to the depths of my self, I produce a translation of the mantra; it passes forth from my mouth, which amazes the two persons. I cross the street and now, from the left sidewalk, I hear the beautiful woman shouting in order to be heard by me. She tells me her father has authorized her to spend four hours with me, and we can go out walking wherever we want. I don't feel surprised about this, I tell her that I'll come for her in half an hour, to which she responds by kissing me on the mouth. She is a consummately beautiful creature who radiates enchantment. When first I saw her, she occupied the center of the mandala. I have the sensation that after I wake up I am going to see her again, in the future—that a marvelous woman is going to come to me."

My head seems to float in an ocean of sweetness, Helena protects my dream and her touch is balm. Images follow one after another but her fingertips brushing my face tell me that I should not be afraid, that I should go on.

"I see myself in a desert place, it is night and the moon illumi-nates each contour of the grasses and small bushes that grow there. My sensation is of peace and tranquility. Suddenly I see in front of me a wonderfully beautiful woman who smiles, inviting me to approach. Two immense birds flank her, mirroring her every movement. Supremely attractive, she seduces everyone who sees her, but I understand in the dream that being with her would kill me, since she is a goddess, an entity beyond our human level of awareness and feeling. That is the reason why her clothing, the birds as tall as human beings, her face, and her entire body are of gold—flexible and natural, but gold.

She realizes that I love her, that my emotion is true. I see then that around where we are standing, as if protecting us, rise crystal walls that permit us to see the countryside but protect us from everything else. There is a danger in lying down with this woman-goddess; she knows it and tells me to wait a little, she is going to talk to God: now she is Israel. I see her leave the crystal building and I sense in the dis-tance the roar of a storm or earthquake. It is God speaking to her. She implores him to let me be with her without dying due to my mortal condition. The thunder gradually dies out, as if the storm had passed."

I awake very excited and tell Helena about my meeting with the woman of gold. She smiles and caresses my head. The dream has moved me profoundly, the birds, the woman of gold and love who is Israel. Only the sweetness of Helena's fingertips on my temples could have calmed me. Why do you question the mysteries? she says. We come spinning across millions of years, and many phantasms cross our path. There's a sea of surprises at the bottom of your dreams. I can't resist placing my head on her breast again, trying to hear an inaudible melody.

"I go with some other people, all women, on a walk or hike to climb a high mountain. The place is thickly treed and the shrubs, walk-ways, flowers, and so on, are all well cared for.

We have arrived at a guest hostel-cum-temple with bare white walls. Its interior has no special feature beyond the height of the ceil-ings, twice as high, or more, than those of normal rooms. Beatriz and other women, or they may simply be phantoms, are the only compan-

ions I have in this adventure.

Suddenly, upon entering the living room, I sense that all the walls are vibrating, as if expressing something of great importance that is somehow a message for me. I understand then I must do a very special work in each of these empty rooms. This work consists in conceiving or creating a poem that represents the most extreme, particular, essential character of each of these rooms, which all seem merely soothing and exactly the same.

And why have I come here? Why have I climbed the mountain and received the commission to bring about that exact combination and order of sounds and images that can express this place, can be the poem so long awaited? I know I accept this fully, it is my destiny, I must accomplish what time requires of me.

I see myself once again in company with those other, almost un- real, people, and I suggest to them that we go down the mountain the same way we'd come up. An important and wise person indicates that first we have to descend from the peak in a sort of elevator in order later to board a train that winds down along the slopes. The train is yellow, similar to a plastic inflatable life raft, but immense and flexible. It seems that it is the only way to avoid dangers."

"I'm in front of our house in Río Loa, a little to the left side, in the direction of the Miño volcano, and in the dream I see depressions in the terrain. But now I am not there but one or two hundred meters lower down, buried in the interior of the rock. It is difficult to move, impossible to leave. Undoubtedly there has been a catastrophe and I am dead.

I see myself on an operating table in a very narrow room. I feel no emotion. Suddenly two doctors enter, accompanied by a nurse. It surprises me that the first doctor, dressed in white, has the head of a dog. He is brusque, almost brutal. Maybe with his fingers, maybe with hooks, he draws apart the ribs of my upper chest and looks for my heart so that he can rip it out and eat it. He is infuriated, my heart has disap- peared, and although he roughly probes right and left he can't find any- thing inside my chest. Then he goes away.

The other doctor approaches and with a sense of awe I see on his shoulders the immense head of a bird of prey. Like the other, he is en- raged, and drives his beak repeatedly into my jaw, extracting my teeth as if they were kernels of corn. My mouth is empty but he remains furious, for now in my jaw there are metal teeth that he cannot devour.

He leaves my jaw in pieces and tells me angrily that myriads of centuries will pass before I will succeed in returning to the upper level of the earth's crust.

When both doctors have retired, the nurse approaches; she is now wrapped in bandages that literally cover her from head to foot. She is faceless, and only her arms, though also enshrouded, can move freely. She holds some kind of wooden box, and I don't know how but she pulls off my penis and testicles. She is the only one who has found something in me. She goes away like a shadow, the shadow without end where I am submerged forever.

I think to myself that on the earth's surface there are fissures, and then slowly I mutter verses of a poem, the only thing I can do. The verses rise through the fissures of rock and reach that spot in front of the house in Río Loa. It is green there, and I see that the poems take the form of immense blue flowers, almost twenty centimeters across, with five petals, such as are rarely encountered in the desert landscape.

Now a woman dressed in white approaches; I listen to her steps and fear it is the nurse-mummy from there below. Maybe it is, but here she is something beneficent and positive. She looks for water to care for the flowers and let the poems blossom and multiply. They are the 'communicating vessels' with the world below."

I awoke as if from a slumber of many years, although everything was as it had been and my head was resting on Helena's belly. I try to sit up and feel her holding me against her chest, tenderly, possessor of an eternal wisdom.

Dear Ludwig, she says, don't you realize I've looked for you in many forms? I've taken a thousand faces, I've traveled empty roads to arrive here and have you in my arms. I'm all the women you imagine, the eternal feminine pulsating around you, the impossible that you look for, that every phantasm is a form of. I'm the "mystical lover" in that painting by Susana where a young naked woman opens her chest and shows her heart engraved with some of your verses. That's why the dog didn't find his food: it was somewhere else, inside my own chest. I'm the woman covered in bandages who descends into the rock and steals your penis and testicles, as Isis did to Osiris—but I do it to protect you. I do it so that despite catastrophe the marvelous man can be saved, the man who brings flowers, muttering verses, and wakes me so I can come to meet him, be at your side, be the pillow with blue petals on which you dream.

I felt wind stirring the old pepper trees. Time had entered another dimension and each particle of this instant was precious and eternal. Sitting now beside Helena, I looked into her eyes. There were no flames anymore, only the current of the river that flows in the glances of those who love each other. Words failed; clearly all the universe was gathered in this feminine presence.

Double Wedding with Disguises

he time on the porch had passed like a gust of wind. The laughter and talking of my brother and sisters carried me back again to reality. It appeared that, though few had been invited, the whole village was going to attend Elvira and Sixto's wedding. It was a celebration not dictated by the calendar and everybody wanted to see how things would fall out.

Elvira's house, located in the village center, was small and my father had asked the Maestro to help organize the event, though he objected that he was not an expert in marriage customs. My mother and Señora Rosario were making a wedding cake for the sweethearts, and everyone else had to accept the work assigned. Since I was on a visit, I was free of all obligation and could chat with my laughing brother and sisters.

Katty sat down with Helena and me on the porch and voiced her doubts about the wedding's success. Yesterday, she said, Sixto's happiness was obvious to everyone, but now—I talked to him just an hour ago and he seemed worried, frightened by bad omens. He had a dream at dawn that left him distracted. I insisted for a long time and finally he told me:

"Katty, I don't exactly know what's happening to me. I'm mad for Elvira, but everything about marriage is so frightening, I'm in anguish. I'm not sure whether the priest is coming from Calama, I know his evil character. And besides, this morning they carried the coffin with the body of Doña Tomasa over to him, so I imagine he must be furious with our whole village. Maybe your father and the distinguished gentleman visiting you might agree to be witnesses, or hand us our marriage certificate? Everyone else in the village is happy—Siglic is going to give me the rings—but I'm afraid. I don't know exactly what's happening to me. Besides, I had a dream that seemed an evil omen."

"I was walking with a group of other people on a recently paved road. All around flowers were growing among the branches of the bushes and in the fields. The road was all curves and suddenly I realized as I walked along that I was lost. I could hear the others' voices, some of them laughing, and I called to them but heard only echoes—maybe they heard me, but we couldn't find each other. Finally, growing desperate, I decided to follow the asphalt path. The branches became higher and at many points, which seemed like entrances to a labyrinth, the road divided in two or three directions. Suddenly I heard music and listening intently I realized that it was a wedding march. But I couldn't find the right road: surely Elvira would be very angry with me. Besides, every moment the undergrowth got higher and thicker and I didn't know how I'd ever find my way once night came on. I tried to run, to cry out, but nothing worked.

Somewhere Elvira was waiting for me but I didn't know how to get to her. Such an important day and I had been so foolish as to get lost among these bushes I'd never seen before; they aren't in Río Loa but maybe in some lost broken place reached only by the sound of music."

"Miss Katty, I don't know what to do. If you can, help me."

My sister had promised to, but she really didn't know what could be done. The only thing we were sure of was that the rather informal wedding would be presided over by the Maestro and my father, who would function as ministers since no one expected anymore that the priest would show up. Each person invited would bring along a dish of food for the party, which made me smile, since in Canada, where I'd lived for so many years, the parties are often that way: each person brings the drink that he or she likes or a food that is a personal favorite to share with everyone else.

It was beginning to get dark, so I walked Helena to her lodgings; she wanted to put on a dress I hadn't seen before. We agreed I would come for her in an hour so we could go together to the wedding. In the neighborhood I saw those diminutive devils, the children of the pious Inés Sarabia, galloping around on their immense ostriches. There was no trick or prank, no matter how dangerous, that they weren't inclined to try.

Well, you three, I said sarcastically, have they invited you to the wedding even though you're not adults? Naturally, they replied in chorus, and we've even practiced a few vaudeville turns to entertain those present. I imagined the evil little hoaxes they were preparing and walked home to be alone for a while and put my thoughts in order. Warm evening air, a soft breeze, and the immense ringed moon rising on the horizon offered anyone who could feel and contemplate them that magic which light reflected on objects communicates. I sat down on the porch hammock and closed my eyes so as to look at the image of Helena beneath my eyelids. All was tranquil; the wind gliding smoothly over the sands produced those tricks of serpentine design that extend into waves and tell the secrets of the desert.

Many a Río Loa gentleman had had his heart broken by Elvira's charms and it was an open secret that Father was one of them. Still, events didn't seem to be affecting him; he was laughing with the Maestro and making jokes about the whole business. Everything necessary was being prepared in the bride's house, and after the wedding those who wished to dance would be able to go to the club, which was more spacious. There everyone would have the chance to celebrate with the newlyweds or recall similar doings of the past.

Mother passed by with the other ladies who had taken charge of the reception arrangements, and told me amusedly that Asmodeus had unloaded various boxes he had brought as gifts for the whole village. They contained so many costumes that there was no end to the possible choices. Asmodeus the Old One now arrived from the general store where he had established himself. He and Juan Siglic were bringing in the costumes and opining on how those for whom they were intended would like them. Everything was—in his words—in a real hurly-burly.

It seemed to me a great stroke: unusual for a wedding, but who could resist assuming a new identity armed with a splendid mask? I showered quickly, and a little later when I passed the general store I saw Asmodeus carrying more boxes toward our house. Don't disturb the dream of poets! he shouted ingratiatingly. Here's your costume, made to order. He laughed as he passed out other boxes to my sisters, who took turns guessing what disguise Asmodeus himself would don. Everyone seemed happy and intent on the party about to begin. A few minutes before, a truckload of musicians had arrived from Calama; no one knew who had hired them. But in every little town, musicians come like bees to honey—or rather, to the liquor that usually flows at these celebrations.

Rapidly I put on my costume, a black suit with a lace collar like those worn centuries ago by Spanish grandees, with some accessories to give it greater realism: a sword with a guard of Philippine coral, and a blue sash embroidered with ingenious decorative devices. Truly the suit did seem made to order; I put on the hat and attached mask and hurried to Helena, who must have been waiting for me for a long time. Or so I thought, according to the common illusion men always entertain, for when I called at her door I heard her ask me to wait a little, she was almost ready for the wedding. I sat down on the porch to talk with José Kruger, who perhaps out of nostalgia had chosen a sailor costume. He was happily enthusiastic about the scheduled dancing, which was one of his passions. He told me that at noon he'd gone to Calama to get a coffin to hold Doña Tomasa's body. It had been expensive, but with the help of a carpenter friend he'd been able to assemble it and bring it over in a ramshackle cart. At the Schutt house, the body of the old woman was already stinking terribly, he said with disgust, and putting the body in the box had destroyed the elaborate coiffure of her gray hair, which was difficult to dress again. The hairs had a life of their own; they stuck out through every slit between the boards. Sara the mulatto had lit fires whose fumes were supposed to drive off the spirit of the dead woman and had tied two big rocks to the ankles, which according to her would keep her mother from walking around the village like a soul in torment. I saw her, Kruger said, put two antique coins on the old lady's eyes and a handful of ashes in her mouth, all this with anguished insistence to whoever would listen that as soon as possible the coffin must be taken out of the house. I was watching Gustavo and her from the porch and didn't want to intrude but the carter was insisting we get started and the disagreeable odor was everywhere. The carter and I drove to the church in Calama, and on the way fear seized us both: we thought the dead woman was trying to move her legs— they were striking against the sides of the box. This job scared me; I assure you I did it solely out of friendship for Gustavo.

I tried to calm him: it was broad daylight, when the dead never try to bother the living.

We could tell, Kruger went on, that the priest definitely did not want to receive us, because Doña Tomasa was famous as a witch and besides had never gone to church, much less confessed her sins. When we threatened to leave the coffin right there in front of his church, he decided to order us, cursing us all the while, to put her in a bell tower two or three blocks away, which is not in use. We could leave the corpse there and if someone wanted to visit her, well, the door was open. The place seemed more like a tavern with crosses and dry flowers, but maybe it was what the dead woman would have wanted, and we had done our part. And later we'd accompany the remains to the cemetery and bury her, just as she'd wished.

Kruger and I suspended our talk when Helena appeared, in a relatively simple costume of iridescent velvet, a very elaborate head-dress framing her face. We greeted her with admiration, although, we said, the costume made her seem very serious. She answered lightly that we understood nothing about disguises, that what we saw was only an outer mantle. It opened to reveal a white dress with strings of vibrant color that ended in pearls, in which she looked like an erotic Hindu statue, robed in smooth caressing velvet.

I've ordered the three little ones, she told us, to find an old carriage that will go with our costumes. At that instant Gaspar appeared and with great ceremony addressed Helena: Gracious Majesty, Contessa Ferrucchi, the carriage is at the door to take you, along with these gentlemen, to the wedding. We will escort you on Osuli, Roderroc and Olleb, who have grown accustomed to us. So it was that we climbed into an ancient carriage we had never seen before and were driven through the village, escorted by the little devils laughing on their giant ostriches. The eyes of the horses, ringed with red, shone in the darkness.

Quickly we found ourselves in the village center, surrounded by curious people we could not recognize at all, now that they had hidden themselves behind masks. I leapt to the ground and held out my hand to Helena, more attractive than ever in the moonlight. Kruger got down and plunged into the crowd to find one of my sisters and engage her for the dance after the wedding.

Helena and I, arm in arm, entered the small house and in every room met six or eight persons who, unable to recognize us, greeted us with a nod. What seemed odd to me, in this tiny house that I knew well, was that we passed through one after another of these dimly lit rooms and I did not recognize any of them. After having crossed five or six, we entered the main room, brilliantly illuminated and, in contrast with the bareness of the others, hung with tapestries in vibrant colors. There, before a rectangular table, were Father and the Maestro, waiting for the engaged couple.

A few minutes later we saw the resplendent pair arrive, she in a white wedding gown on which multitudinous flowers moved with the light, Sixto, the groom, wearing a decorous dark suit and shoes with heels that added centimeters to his height. The musicians interrupted their saraband and the noise died out completely.

The bridal couple having knelt down on a prie-dieu provided with two thick cushions, the Maestro addressed the gathering: This is not a role I play frequently, so I beg your pardon for any small errors. I and my friend, Guillermo Zeller, who have not seen each other for many decades, are going to officiate here as solemn witnesses for this wedding which will join Elvira Ossorio and Sixto Lora Canto as husband and wife. My father now went and stood in front of the betrothed and asked them in a solemn tone we had rarely heard from him: Dear Elvira, do you take Sixto as your husband? She hesitated an instant and then responded with a tuneful yes. The Maestro directed the same question to Sixto Lora and he, a little confused, maybe nervous, seemed not to understand. The Maestro did not repeat it, and when the engaged man finally realized what had been asked, he responded that yes, he was delighted.

The musicians resumed playing their instruments while the couple exchanged metal rings. The Maestro and Father offered felicitations, as required, and embracing them suggested that all head for the club where the reception would be held. As we were forming up in a happy caravan to leave for the dance, the bride threw the spray of flowers in her hand high into the air. By I don't know what strange principle of physics the bouquet flew to Helena who caught it in her fingers. Everyone laughed and congratulated themselves that there were candidates who might repeat the ceremony. Asmodeus then appeared with an enormous tray and served everyone a delicious, exalting liquor. I touched my glass to Helena's and the crystal bell we had heard on previous occasions sounded again. The armadillo, next to my ear, said to me: Cross your arm and drink, each of you, from the glass in the other's hand. I took his counsel and, following the Russian custom, threw the emptied glass, which shattered against a wall. "Love," said the faithful translator, "is the only multiple ceremony."

Maestro Leonardo now passed us a cushion bearing two heavy rings, with a text in gold on the inner surface to encircle the ring finger. On both the writing repeated identical verses of an anonymous poet.

"To sing, to flow from glass to glass burning

I let down your hair like a river
If only I could drink you from inside your skin
And we could go out through the drunken bells of the
    rain..."

We put the rings on one another and I saw Father and the Maestro, not without a certain emotion, clapping each other on the back and laughing. I kissed Helena and the taste of her lips communicated a sweetness known only in dreams. Then we followed the crowd, which was eager to dance and cut capers in the streets, to the club, where the musicians had set themselves up to give, here and now, their supreme performance.

Though not an accomplished dancer, I believe that dancing with the beloved is an exercise in levitation based on music. Helena had removed her dark mantle and shone like a living, seductive statue, and so a great advantage was given to me in this matter of dancing. Revolving like butterflies, we watched one couple after another in the salon remove their masks out of curiosity. Some were happy when they did it, others were a little disconsolate at having made an error. But the celebration and Asmodeus' drinks put a good face on things for even the most hardhearted inquisitor.

After dancing for a while, Helena and I decided to get away by ourselves, as any couple wants to do in such a situation. By now everyone was so drunk that we needed no artifice to pass unnoticed. Outside we ran into the three devils, but Helena gestured that we wanted to be alone and we climbed into the old carriage that had brought us, telling the invisible coachman to drive to the Valley of the Moon. There, at last, we'd be left in peace. When we arrived at the Salar, my adorable accomplice ordered the carriage back to Río Loa. I know where I am, she said; maybe we'll go back tomorrow.

Now that we were alone, Helena, who shone more beautifully than ever, insisted on asking me if I was happy. It isn't the salt, or the moonlight, I told her, it's you who've enveloped me in this mad love. Pressing her tiny shoes against a metal surface there in the sand, she motioned to me to lift it. Though it was a solid plate, it didn't seem heavy and opened to reveal at our feet a descending stair. We closed the door behind us. In the lunar radiance that salt produces under the least glimmer of light, we went down almost a hundred steps, which brought us to the gate of a garden full of flowers. The ocean must have been very near, because we heard the breaking of waves on rocky cliffs.

How much time had gone by? Had years passed since we had arrived? Would there be someone waiting for us there? We knew nothing.

I felt the poverty that wishing to speak such thoughts to the beloved woman always reveals in words. Verses written a thousand years ago flowered in my memory.

"Sometimes I would like to summon you in dreams
As when you pass tinted with oxide from the million wings
Of butterflies that wove your mantle as queen of the sun
In zithers that are skin in the beehives
Where you store the fruit that each day drives me mad
When you open your legs slightly in the locusts' game
But you have already leapt you are living deep within
My forehead where you've made your nest with fleece
Warmer than the blood in whose form you constantly
   flow
Like fire in water from one glass to another
With the hinge of your legs you make a swift cross
Scissors that signify tiger among the pillows."

Oh, don't you understand yet, said Helena, lying back on a bed of petals, that I've looked for you wearing many different women's faces? Yes, I remember those verses written on the margin of death. It was a sweet, melancholy summer, in that old house in Agincourt, when you believed nothing ever returns. Over and over again I appeared in your dreams. I tried to drink from your lips as I'm doing now, but that was a different dimension, when symbols seemed to keep transmuting themselves and many nightmares confronted you.

Yes, I told her, I have seen you in my dreams. And here's a coincidence, darling, that may interest you, or make you smile at least. Do you know that the woman who helped me decipher my dreams years ago has your very name? We knew her as Doctor Hoffman, from the last name of her husband, but she was born Helena Jacobi—for her close friends, simply Lola. Our beloved Lola.

I saw Helena smile: Yes, now and then I'm behind the face of every woman. How often reading your dreams has taken me down the indecipherable road where I found you! Sometimes the feeling of love can steal our breath away. Now let's go walk on the beach: there's an interior sea here that not many people know about, and we'll live on its shore. I saw her look toward the waves and I kissed her eyelids, which were moist.

A Stormy Burial

t was hard to think of going back: that indefinable time spent with Helena occupied all my mind. She said tenderly: Ludwig, the lover is never separated from the beloved; even when I'm at your side in an invisible form, you only have to say my name for me to be present. The day was already well advanced when I dropped her off at the guest hostel.

I left Helena to rest and walked home, where strong coffee and a shower brought me back to reality. The heat had begun and in the distance I could already see the deceptive waters that lead travelers astray. My brother and sisters, in animated conversation on the porch as usual, greeted me airily and told me I'd missed the best of the party.

If only you'd seen, they said, the comedy of errors that occurred last night. The costumes, along with Asmodeus' wonderful drinks, threw confusion into the dancers, and Sixto too, after finishing with the cake ceremony and drinking every toast the guests offered, had lost his head and gotten confused about who was who. It hadn't seemed peculiar at the time, since more or less the same thing was happening to almost everyone. The night passed. At dawn he went to look for Elvira but couldn't find her. Disorder reached its height when, hours later, the sun already high, they found him in the Durands' corral, asleep next to a llama. He explained that, maybe due to the liquor, he had believed he was enjoying the pleasures of Elvira's love. He then went to her house and found her sleeping; when she woke she was a bit put out to see him.

My brother and sisters supposed, from the solemn manner Father had assumed for the ceremony, that it was he who danced out of the hall with Elvira. Everyone took it as a joke and he had claimed that's what it was; but clearly he'd taken advantage of the costumes and hilarity to place her bridegroom in a deep trance. Carlos and our sisters had tried to get the whole story out of him but he would only laugh and say that Elvira couldn't sleep alone on her wedding night. That clod Sixto hadn't appeared, and since the costumes and darkness leant themselves to misrule, he had dedicated himself to love until the sun signaled it was best to retire. Mother had laughed at the whole thing. In this "mistake," she'd said, there was longing and calculation on Guillermo's side and on Elvira's, since it takes two to tango, and in making love it's natural to remove your disguise.

And everyone had smiled along with her and agreed.

Ida went on: But Elvira's mother (Doña Lucrecia was the woman's name) had penetrated the appearances and she came to demand repayment from Mother for a small pitcher which, according to her, Father must have broken while in her house. Mother knew nothing about it, but just then little Gaspar, Judith and Salome presented themselves for breakfast, and they convinced Doña Lucrecia to go with them because they knew where the pitcher could be found. Tricked by their promises, the clumsy old lady agreed to mount one of the ostriches. She left with those rascals and was soon being run all over the neighborhood and village. The pitcher, the pitcher, she cried despairingly, bouncing up and down on the back of the giant bird. After hours of trotting around, her only desire was to get off, but she was nailed to the saddle as if by enchantment. The coarse jokes and innuendoes the villagers made at her expense had no effect. The fact was that she just could not get off the ostrich.

My mother offered us a light noontime meal and soon we were in the dining room, recalling and laughing over the events of recent days. Imagine, said Ida, Señorita Zoila danced for hours after the wedding. And Siglic? And Kruger? I asked absently. Kuni said that the whole village must have been taking dance lessons in secret, since they had performed skillfully and elegantly to every type of music. And Father? I asked. You know he's never been an ace dancer, they told me, but something—the effects of love or Asmodeus' liquor or Elvira's charms—sent him gliding through all the steps, there was no holding him back. We laughed our surprise over Father, who had always been entirely hopeless at dancing.

While we were talking, the Rossos arrived, circumspect as befitted their gleaming gray automobile. They wanted to know what time was set for Doña Tomasa's burial. We didn't know for sure but thought the best idea would be to set out for Calama in order to spend a moment in the bell tower outfitted for the laying out, and from there join the funeral procession. This seemed reasonable to everyone, so I put on a lightweight suit and a hat to protect me from the sun and we went down to the square, where we found buses hired by Gustavo Schutt waiting to take people to Calama, though many, with a more active spirit, preferred to walk over; the deceased wasn't well liked by the villagers, but still her burial was going to be a real social event. Father had remained behind to invite the Maestro, if he would consider attending, and Helena and Asmodeus. And everyone was sure the three devils on their respective ostriches would show up, since they never let such an event pass them by, above all if there was a chance of doing mischief.

Calama is a small town that probably existed when the Spanish arrived—at least the mayor always said so—but although it was situated in a green valley watered by the river, the omnipresent dust seriously diminished its charm. Father told the Maestro that at the beginning of the century, when he had first arrived at Calama, it was raining, and this, surprisingly, seemed to be considered by the inhabitants as a disaster. Now, only a day since it had snowed in the desert, the little town was still struggling to get its feet under it.

The buses took us directly to the bell tower, where a dozen curiosity seekers had gathered. Apparently that morning Sara the mulatto had come and washed and swept the place, installed four enormous curtains, and put some flowers around. These last were very difficult to obtain, and for other funerals were made out of crepe paper on the eve of the wake. But since the eve of this wake had coincided with the wedding night, no one had had time to make wreaths and flowers, so we had to content ourselves with bringing some green branches with colored ribbons.

The priest of Calama was indeed very disagreeable; he told the town official that it would be best to bury the dead woman in the old abandoned Cemetery of the Plague Victims, since he couldn't swear that she was even a Christian. The coffin was placed on a gun carriage pulled by two horses, and a large procession, in small groups or in couples, followed the dead woman on her last journey: more than a hundred people had come to attend the funeral.

The long line formed up to leave by one of the principal streets and near the end of it we stood: my brother and sisters and I, Kruger, and the two Spaniards, Bilbao and Zamarreño, who always, whenever there was the slightest occasion, disagreed with each other. My father and the Maestro were last in line; the Maestro, who always showed good humor no matter how he was tried, professed himself eager for the three-kilometer walk that awaited.

I had seen in the native villages of Mexico how an orchestra brightens up a funeral procession, but in this case there was no music, and everyone walked in silence or making comments, not always generous, about the dead woman on the wagon.

On leaving the town we noticed that, though the road wasn't suitable for dancing, muffled noises were coming from inside the coffin. And as this was not a deluxe item, we saw strands of white hair sprouting from between its gapped boards and growing before our eyes until they touched the ground. Gustavo and Sara tried to pass off the event, but soon the disagreeable odor of the corpse was joined by the cackling voice of Doña Tomasa insulting those in attendance one after another.

"And you, Sara, like Potiphar's wife, what will you do now? Surely the only thing that you learned in life was to wallow in men's arms. And that Gustavo, hiding himself there, why didn't he bring his mandolin? I know I'm no favorite of his, but out of respect at least. Ha, ha, and those Rossos, solemn as ever. Assunta, fat as a cow, quit beating yourself with Ernesto's lash."

As moment by moment the insults grew more violent, mourners dropped away from the procession, certain that Doña Tomasa was a damned soul whose viper tongue would pursue them with vilification. When the group had been reduced almost by half, so that we were only a few meters from the hearse, we could clearly hear the deceased's insults and insolent slurs. Father approached to see what was happening and the cackling voice asked him: "How are you, dirty old man? Isn't it true that you've been sleeping with Elvira for years? And that old idiot on an ostrich demanding pay for her pitcher. How well I know you all."

Suddenly we saw the Maestro approach, and the voice modulated into one long cry of fear. "Mercy, mercy on this sad old crone, your lordship. Allow me peace beneath the blessed ground of this cemetery." But Leonardo, seeming deaf to her prayers, struck the coffin with the edge of his ring and instantly the noises were heard no more. We had arrived at the old abandoned cemetery and two or three people went to look for a still unoccupied grave where we could put the coffin. There was one at the back, and toward it we headed. Maybe because of the heat, the nauseating odor of the corpse had become still stronger. The coffin was lowered by ropes into the ground and Doctor Sarabia, with one of those oratorical bursts that frequently occur in persons who believe in rhetoric, said: "We are united here in joy. So many miracles have occurred in this town that burying Doña Tomasa can't help but be a good sign for all of us. I wish her quiet, virtue, all that she never had in this life."

He took a handful of sand, which he let fall on the wooden box. It hadn't, to tell the truth, been a model funeral eulogy, but everyone was grateful for its brevity. Each came up to throw a handful of earth into the grave and soon two husky workers covered the spot with boards, installing also a rough cross made of two wooden slats that had been left in the place. There was nothing there we could use to write the name of the dead woman, but the sticks had stamped on them in painted letters, "Río Loa" and "Danger, dynamite inside." We thought this would make it easy for the relatives to identify the grave, in case anyone was ever crazy enough to look for it.

Slowly we left the cemetery. Outside we encountered Elvira's mother, still mounted on an ostrich and screeching like a magpie. The Maestro, putting his hand on my arm, said, How delightful it is that this ceremony of birth or dying is always being repeated. Motioning to Gaspar, he made that devil help the old woman down, now that her bones were fused from riding bareback on the elegant Osuli. She tripped over her tongue, trying to thank him, but not a word came out.

My sisters and Carlos, who had remained a little apart, told me that in an open grave, among bones and rags, they had found the glasses that Doctor Sarabia lost. They ran to him to return them, but he made ambiguous gestures, for he was still trying to see to it that Inés not realize what had happened. She was with him, but was so involved in telling Señora Garzón a series of miracles that she paid no attention to such a trivial event as the discovery of a pair of glasses.

Thus it was that Doña Tomasa managed to avoid being laid out on the Zellers' kitchen table, which she had always seen as the gate of hell. Maybe the snowfall had made it easier for her to leave our village and pass through those adobe walls beyond which the other life begins.

The Tarot Cards

erhaps the heat that reverberates in the desert, that warms the rocks, made our journey back to the house longer. The cemetery wasn't far but something in the air weighed on us, making us think serious thoughts. Most of the mourners were dispersed now and the group was reduced to my family and a few friends, like Kruger, Gustavo Schutt and his wife, who didn't want to return home, the Sarabias, Zoila Campana, the Maestro and the three devils, who galloped all around us.

When we arrived at our front porch we were happy to find Mother and Helena waiting with refreshments. It seemed to them we had already moved around more than usual and needed a little rest. There wasn't any objection to such a considerate welcome.

Relaxing on the willow and bamboo porch furniture, we could see with fresh eyes the hours we had just lived through. Helena sat on the arm of my chair and her nearness awoke all my memories of the previous night: her perfume, her way of moving, the tone of her voice that had become a balm transporting me to another universe. Everything happening around me—my father talking with Leonardo about cults in Indonesia, my sisters' jokes—all was absorbed into this passion that enveloped me.

You understand, Guillermo, the Maestro was saying to Father, that good and evil are one and the same entity: that's the mystery of the universe, which the human race has been trying to solve with tunnel vision for scarcely ten millennia. Religions and cults repeat, solidify the

imagery of dreams, and dreams are something more than the linea-
ments of unsatisfied desires. One would say that at times people don't
take account of the brevity, the fragility of life. And everything black
and white, always the same errors repeating themselves to the point of
weariness.

If at times the Maestro was tired, maybe it was disgust at the
weaknesses of those around him that pitched him into his profound
melancholies. I looked at his face and felt compassion for the loneliness
he had to confront throughout the ages, in other faces, other languages,
other customs. Turning to Helena, I spoke this emotion and she con-
fessed to me that she had accompanied him over the long years in part
to temper his loneliness. Few ever succeed in understanding him this
way, she told me, and I love you because for years I've been watching
that compassion in you, your freedom to confront the unknown, the
invisible.

I believe in magic, said Sara the mulatto, because I've seen its
effects. It's the ultimate power, whose force is concentrated in sex: I'm
sure that sex moves the world. Seeing her thus, in the fullness of her
carnality, it wasn't difficult to believe in the sincerity of her words. Be-
sides, she continued, there's something irresistible that carries us to the
satisfying of our desires. I don't know how others do it, but my grand-
mother, who came from Africa, thought that if you took a cord, tied a
knot corresponding to the name of the man you wanted, and struck it,
he would come to you alone—just as if the spirits sent him to plead
with you even though he himself didn't feel a jot of passion. Gustavo
looked at her and I suppose he was putting together in his mind an
image of the sensual Sara striking a knotted cord and repeating his name.

Since the conversation had turned rather frank, Inés and Doctor
Sarabia assured us that they had urgent things to do. Mother had some
little arrangements to make with them and accompanied them to their
house.

It was then that, taking Helena's hand, I asked the Maestro: I
realize you know almost everything about us and our destiny, but we
know so little about you. I'd like you to answer some questions I've
never before dared to put to myself. I understand that they aren't novel,
but if I can call you my friend, and you could come with me to this
village where I spent my childhood, can't you answer simply, so that I
can understand, even if only for the space of one flash of light? What is
our destiny?

The Maestro smiled. His face in the light was beautiful and sorrowful. He said: What do you prefer, that I really answer you with simple words, or that here, in front of everybody, we perform the archaic ceremony of seeing ourselves in the cards?

Something inside of me decided in favor of the tarot, and I replied, clearing the table, that I wanted to exchange and interpret the cards. Then the Maestro passed his hand over the table and it was covered with sand that moved slowly as if under the impulse of the wind.

From the inner pocket of his cape he took a parchment deck and asked Helena to shuffle. Then each person cut the deck, which was placed face down on the sand. I saw that the painted backs of the cards were in fact alive, displaying a vast number of human beings in the most varied occupations. Now, Leonardo indicated to me, each of us, one at a time, should take a card and formulate a question based on it.

Everyone crowded to the table, eager to watch what was happening. I put my hand on the moving sand and took my first card. The Arcanum Six, of the two roads, or love. The Maestro smiled and said, Why charge me with explaining something that in itself is inexplicable? He looked at Helena who, bent over the table, seemed absorbed in the game. You're lucky, he said. Here at last a cycle is completed and after so many avatars Helena will be with you until the end of time. We're born of woman in a chain that no one remembers, and in every life we encounter beings that more or less approximate an image we carry inside us—a type of mirror to which you show yourself many times and in which you are often mistaken. Helena has been following you for two centuries and when I found her in Italy more than a hundred years ago, a painter with a certain likeness to you was showing himself to his mirror. But he saw an illusion, like the rocks and water he painted. I was his friend, but he never understood my feelings and you can see me there in his works, playing the violin, in the role of death in one of his self-portraits. This fleshless skeleton: it's an expression of not understanding what each of us carries inside. I think he never saw my face, the true thirst that consumes me. All the women you love you will find in Helena, and every face you see in this mirror will have her eyes, only her eyes, which have cried so much, waiting for you.

And the ivory book you gave me?

Ay, dear friend! he said, don't you understand that across a multitude of forms, the pheasants are always flying to the same garden, in which you love and are truly at home?

I looked at the card one more time, caressing it between my fingers, and I saw faces appearing that I had almost forgotten: my mother's from when I was small, the faces of so many other women adorned at times with exotic costumes as if they were from the east or the high Himalayas. I thought that he had responded wisely about the card and I signaled him to take a turn.

I watched Leonardo extend his delicate hand, jewels gleaming on his fingers, and turn his card face up: The Old Man, the Hermit.

My sisters in chorus with Zoila Campana exclaimed: That can't be right—he's an elegant gentleman, full of youth!

I regret deceiving you, dear ladies, but this game enters zones where the eye is fooled. I can indeed be the solitary hermit, among other things, since I've lived untold years and like each of you I've come traveling through many lifetimes. The only difference between us is that "I recall myself and this is nostalgia," he said, and I recognized he was quoting the poet Enrique Gómez-Correa. Because good is inseparable from evil, he continued, and they live inside each person from the beginning of time. Leonardo closed his eyes as if summoning an image. Men want good but they do evil; they try to make puppets of them both, and gods and devils multiply. As long as an equilibrium does not exist in human thought, for each Fra Angelico there will be a Hieronymus Bosch. It's unavoidable, necessary, to conceive of being in its unity. I would like... The phrase hung suspended in the air.

With a gesture, he indicated it was my turn again.

I looked at the faces of my family, my friends, Helena. And leaving everything to chance, I reached out my hand and took a card. Even before looking at it I heard the others saying, The Wheel of Fortune. There indeed between my fingers was the ambivalent luck that casts down some while it raises others. I want this for you, the Maestro said. I've desired it for you through several lifetimes: that you should take down walls, that you should destroy the cold and bureaucratic days and years. If with Helena you've arrived at last at making your dreams come true, love will give you good fortune: it's nearer than you imagine.

Mother had returned meanwhile and with Asmodeus' help she brought us large trays of refreshments. You're all so serious, she said. As if your whole life depended on a deck of cards.

I had no question to ask because fortune is something we know nothing about, which is given us as a blessing, a grace, a free gift. I looked at the card and saw that the woman moving the wheel resembled Dürer's Lady Fortuna, only now she was alive, looking into my eyes and smiling.

Leonardo took the deck and with the elaborate gesture of a magician put down the Arcanum Fifteen, The Devil. Then he looked at all of us, as if asking what we wanted to know.

Since nobody else spoke, I said: There are some other things I still want to consult you about. Above all I'd like to know why your apparition in my dreams produced such horror in me. Also, it seems your face has changed over the years.

It's because your image of me is your own interior demon, said Leonardo. As you've become more mature and learned to balance your feelings, you've sensed me as a more human companion who can be you yourself, or your likeness. I had recorded dreams for long periods of my life and knew his reply corresponded to fact.

But if God is unity and you're his counterpart, I said, how is it possible that the infernal always emerges as artificial and monstrous? Isn't that what artists like Picasso or Kafka show? I make collage. Create a balance of contraries...it's difficult, I don't know if I could achieve it. This comment excited Leonardo. It's clear that art and life are in great part a collage, he said. But why not try for a unity that comes not from reason but from something biological and irrational? I know those pieces of yours where you mixed texts of poems with fragments of paintings and cutouts. I don't know what you called them, I believe it was "images and words." There's the key to this irrational, convulsive unity.

I scarcely remembered the experiment; I'd done it years before and it must have been lost someplace in my workshop. This clairvoyance moved me so strongly to penetrate some of the Maestro's mythical qualities that I didn't hesitate to keep questioning him. There's a book of some thousand pages written on this very theme, I said, by Jan Potocki, who lets the fear that possessed him shine through the fluency of his style. And what about the text of Mikhail A. Bulgakov, dear Leonardo—isn't there some of the truth about you in it?

Something of the truth exists in everything. Certainly Jan Potocki talked with me once, but it was on one of his voyages as ambassador to China that we met, on the border of Mongolia. His vision of southern Spain is dominated by period folklore, and those Moorish sisters who appear in his stories correspond in fact to a Christian concept of love that doesn't comprehend some of its aspects. He lived in great torment without finding that balance we were just speaking about. His romantic suicide can't be justified, nor his superstition, which made him polish the small-bore silver bullet that would be fired into his temple. It's as if after many years the terrors of childhood had beset a man grown old.

It was evident from Leonardo's tone that he had a certain sympathy for the Polish count and his voluminous *Manuscript Found in Zaragoza.*

In regard to Mikhail, he said, he was a good friend. Oppressed by a system, he discovered that by making a caricature of me, on the model of Goethe's, he could tell a story very faithful to his dreams and the conversations we had. He enjoyed making caricatures, like all the theatrical crowd, and used some rather cruel brushstrokes on a cat I adopted in Moscow. He asked me to name him and I chose Popota. Your character is similar to his in a lot of ways. He tried to take me from a myth and make me live in that domestic hell the revolutionary Russians planned. The scenes in the theater, although they bored me at times, I did for him. There are places in Moscow we visited together, and their remembrance still fills me with emotion. He laughed: You'd get along well with him.

I sensed that Leonardo had become nostalgic and tried to talk about something else, to let the symbolism of the cards drop.
But he went on: You know, I thought that once you wanted to write about the Galilean. I can tell you one thing, no one understood what he was writing in the sand. They saw their own failures, because their lives were imprisoned inside them. If there's one important thing I can say, it's that despite all the exegesis the world continues to ignore him, and if he were born again, I assure you, they would crucify him again.

There was pain in his eyes. Write something, he said. The sand covers it at times, but later it reappears in other tongues. So with my finger on the table I wrote:

> "The weavers of desire hear the thread running
> Toward your eyes where coals burn decomposing into
>   feathers."

I saw the words dancing in the sand and then a little spiral of wind swept the surface clean, carrying off earth and verses into the air.

I proposed a toast to Leonardo, our charming friend, who had chosen to spend a few days in the small world of Río Loa, so small at times that it was only a tiny space covered with dust. Concerning the Maestro, we knew the mighty works that were in his power, but now we wished only to celebrate the friend. Mother brought a liquor of dried tamarinds and said to him: I want to thank you as a woman and mother for having brought my son to my arms this one time more. Destiny's like the sand blown away by the wind; some see the cards and some ignore them. Your health, dear Leonardo. It's been a pleasure for me to have you visiting with us—your health! Your health! we all repeated together. I saw the eyelids of our guest grow moist.

The Dance— Preparations and Dreams

hen it was late and almost everyone had said good-bye and gone home, we saw the moon rising over the high peaks of the mountain range. My parents and brother and sisters seemed a little melancholy that the day was ending. We had been granted so many varied events, our talk had been so harmonious, that it hurt to think of bringing the day to a close.

It was then that Leonardo, turning to me, said: I've heard you more than once expressing your desires, and I'd like to give you a little gift—something rather ordinary, since a man who finds love wants little else. But you always talk about a party that you'd give if you had so much money that it jingled and you could extend invitations without limit. The only thing that counts is for you to feel happy. You invited me to this village where I've found friends in everyone. Sleep on it tonight, on Helena's soft breast, and let me know tomorrow; the moon's full and I can only stay with you a few more days. He said good night and we watched him cross the street with Father to the Sarabias' house. My brother and sisters had heard me fantasize this way: "If only I had a million dollars and I could invite all my friends to one great party." And they'd always laugh when I began choosing the sites I might like for this party: "The blue mosque in Istanbul, or a grand hotel on Isla Mujeres; the Alcazar in Granada, in the middle of the gardens; or a palace at the very center of the desert."

It seems, they all said at once, that your dreams are coming true; everything's arranged. But we beg you, don't forget to invite us. They made comic signs to Helena, that when the occasion arrived she should remind me of them, or make sure they were present.

Siglic offered to escort Zoila Campana, "since she lived right nearby," and Kruger went off with Gustavo Schutt and Sara, who were a little reluctant to return to their house. My mother said to my brother and sisters: Lovers usually want to be alone when they tell each other secrets in the moonlight. She looked at us with a smile and took the arm of my father, who had returned from the Sarabias'. Sweet dreams, she said, the night's long and the wind's starting to scatter secrets across the desert.

I laughed at her discreet way of putting it; taking Helena's arm, I offered to walk her home. I had so much to ask her, and her presence was as essential to me as the beloved always is for one who loves beyond all measure: such, it seems, has always been my way.

We went out, then, across the sand that the wind was shaping into waves—the closest thing there is to walking on water. Arm in arm, we saw our shadows form a single entity, and any other path would have seemed rough compared to the one now calling us.

Helena asked me: What are you going to ask the Maestro for? I thought about all those immense gatherings at which each person is actually alone with a partner, and I answered: It's a fact that when something seems out of reach, or impossible, one daydreams, making monstrous plans, but on the plane of reality, the most wonderful thing is a gathering where almost everyone knows each other and we share joy with the ones we love. And then there are those who just like to talk and keep in the background, listening to a music no one else can hear. My beloved laughed: What you mean is you want a simple party, where only the feelings speak.

She sat down on a sofa and had me lie with my head on her lap, and while she passed her fingertips over my eyelids I heard her murmur a song. Ludwig dear, she said, remember that there are no frontiers between one world and another. The people you want will come: so the Maestro has decided.

But Helena, what if some of them never met each other in life?

That isn't our concern, she answered. The most important thing is that what you desire should make you happy. I felt that a dream, soft and smooth, was carrying me in its current, perhaps for only a brief instant, but when I opened my eyes I found that Helena was caressing my forehead and repeating: You're like a child; what your lips cannot articulate, your dreams tell me. Don't worry. The people invited to your party will be those you most long for in the depth of your soul.

Her lips brushed across mine in a ritual kiss, with the rhythmic cadence of the tides.

Then I saw the bed sheets opened out like sunny beaches that the seafoam caresses, and heard a fountaining up of words now and then interrupted by a breath, and the laughter that bends reeds in the wind. What could I ask for, what should I dream about, if the one I dreamed was here in my arms? There is a rare sweetness that flowers into passion: it is the union of two loving beings like a zone that encircles the universe. Such was Helena with me: she encompassed each particular element of my desires, she remembered long passages in which my being had been synonymous with thirst and she was there to satisfy me, to tell me that the wall is only an illusion, that we were a single being in which the two of us continually drank of each other, augmenting our joy or our delicious torment.

When I woke the sun had been high for hours. Helena was singing a song by Schumann while Asmodeus, with a gravity I hadn't before seen in him, accompanied her on the piano.

I've never experienced a better way to wake up, I told them. Helena was radiant. Asmodeus, whom I embraced enthusiastically, felt thin and fragile to me, and timid, like someone surprised in a misdeed.

We went to the kitchen only to discover that the chocolate had run out and we would have to console ourselves with a scrap of almond cake and black coffee. Asmodeus was in a strange mood; he told me how it bothered him that people looked on him as a sort of exotic animal; he'd always been sensitive and who can resist music, that poetry made of sounds? We agreed about this: especially, we said, when the vibration of the human voice adds to the instruments that warmth which comprehends every degree of feeling and thought. I know you love her, Asmodeus said, referring to Helena, but when she sings, she produces an enchantment that stirs the soul. I said I thought so too, and he, as if fearful he had gone too far with his compliments, said that many tasks awaited him, since everything had to be ready for the dance by the time the moon's ivory face began to mount the sky.

We saw him walk off, taking along the little devils on their giant ostriches. The air was utterly motionless, no sound disturbed the quiet. Helena wanted to know what I had done in the village when I was a child. She took a big parasol that was standing in a corner and we went out walking on the pampa, which is the name the villagers have given the desert. We hiked several kilometers beyond my parents' house and with a certain emotion I pointed out to her the paths that I and other children had created on the "desert's pavement," simply moving to the sides the pebbles in a segment forty centimeters wide and using them as borders. It had often been possible to trace very intricate designs on that crystallized terrain where no moisture but wine ever runs: the results of our play had persisted there for years and years. Yes, I was moved, showing them to Helena; and surely it had been an impossible labor, the one we children had also sometimes tried: to make ships of rock, dream vessels which, we believed, our imagination would somehow move.

Helena had grown pensive. Maybe there was some reason in all this, she said. The intricate little paths remind me of the currents in water and the caverns that lie hundreds of meters farther down. You yourself have seen that an interior sea does exist. Then why not try to build a ship that can cross it? Sometimes we merely pass high over a greater knowledge, which is luminous in children, and we don't consider that their dreams are more real, without the adult world's shackles.

I didn't venture to interrupt her: what she said was just what might have come from my own lips. Let's go see your mother, my other self, she said. And I have to talk with the Maestro.

On the porch Carlos and Katty were chatting with the Garzóns. One of the Garzón brothers, Pedro, who had been my schoolfellow, took such delight in reminiscences that we could question him on any of the village's inhabitants, since he knew by heart all about them.

Do you remember the Quiroga sisters? he said to me. They were two lovely girls who used to play with us. Their mother cooked one meal every ten days and buried the food in a hole. Beatriz and Carmen died at almost exactly the same time, before reaching twenty; the mother outlived them by a few months. It seems that the meals got mixed in the hole with poisonous sulphur. Don Pedro, the father, who's still alive, if I'm not mistaken, always says he was saved by the effects of the wine he drank copiously, as an antidote.

And the Durands, what's become of them? I asked.

You know, Pedro told us, that Durand was a great gentleman, gracious and physically powerful. They had, if I recall rightly, two daughters and one little boy. I believe Durand lives now in the interior of the Iquique region; unexpectedly, due to an illness, the wife, who was young, suddenly turned into someone forty to sixty years older than her husband. How she aged from one day to the next, no one knows. The girls,

Inés and Doris, disappeared after an explosion at the dynamite factory; we don't know if it was from horror or some other motive. They were two beauties, about sixteen or seventeen years old; someone said he had run into them once thirty years later on a street in Quito, but they were still the same age, and that maybe their whole story had been an enchantment. The little boy, Juan—his mother used to tie him to a post—when she died he burned the cords she had threatened to bind him with from the sepulcher. Pedro Garzón was often overheated in his judgments, but I remembered the horror I had felt as a child when I saw young Juan fastened to a stake. I had told my mother what I had seen with a certain terror, for fear she would adopt the method, since at times she scolded for misbehaving. I knew Pedro Garzón and his family well. He was more or less the same age as Kuni, and I thought that, if one could make wishes for the dance that night, they would be a good couple.

Mother offered us some snacks and told us by the way that she had seen Asmodeus, in whom she had great confidence, making long lists of liquors, fruits and everything needed for a party. And, she said, there's a lot of activity out near the coast of the Salar Grande. Your father and Leonardo went off early in that direction.

I preferred to avoid the preparations, and I decided, after talking and listening to music, to take a good siesta. Events had taught me to be fresh for whatever might come. I went into my parents' bedroom, where I had dreamed so often, and disposed myself to wait for the dream that would be my light for the rest of the day.

"It appears that we are looking for an apartment to live in. Father and Mother have located one on the upper floors of a building in the center of a city which is celebrating a holiday. We go to a terrace from which the whole area can be seen and I ask Father why he didn't rent the apartment in the center of the terrace. Seemingly a danger exists that I don't know about and Father doesn't stop to explain it to me.

I see many trucks passing and the noise and the traffic can be dangerous. There is such congestion that I do not understand how such a large crowd can circulate in the narrow streets. We decide to leave for the outskirts where there is more space and we can be more tranquil. I notice various children waiting around or playing; I don't take much note of their faces, but my attention is drawn to the bare feet of a little boy seated on a step. The children surround me and explain that they are willing to work free, but they want me at least to pay the 'Maestro.'

(By which they mean, I think, their professor, the master barber.) Then a tall blond man, seemingly in charge of the school, though I am not sure, walks out of the building. He looks like an actor I know, and after greeting me he takes me into one of the rooms. There I have to cut wood with a hatchet. I begin my task at once, trying to chop a log approximately eight centimeters thick that has another, whiter stick inserted into one of its ends with careful workmanship. I try to cut it longitudinally, following the grain, but the man in charge of the school stops me and shows me a number of huge logs piled in the center of the room: these are what must be cut into pieces. I begin to cut them immediately and see that they are very colorless, as if rotten, or mixed into the earth itself. Is this cutting hair?

It appears that I myself am the master barber. The earth and the logs have hot coals in their interior; only now do I notice that the man who was there has placed a sheet around his neck and it reaches to the spot where I am cutting wood. Using a hooked comb, I have to open the sheet down the back, now that the hair has been cut and everything beneath the cloth is burning like red embers. I move the sheet slightly aside and am shocked to see that his back and his whole body are nothing but blood, as if he has no skin. I can tell by some movements he makes that I cause him pain and should work with great care. I do so. He tells me then that he is the previous master barber and that for some unknown reason he burns continually, painfully, in blood. Maybe I am he, I say to myself. The barber's chair—if there is a chair—is continuous with those logs I am chopping apart, which break into flames in the earth."

"I was in Santiago, with Beatriz. We had to go looking for Estela at her house, which was situated in a neighborhood different from the one where, I remember, it really stands. The houses were one story high, gray, surrounded by trees, and among them was a park with a lowered area or a depressed level in its grounds—like the John XXIII Park, but at the back there was a pool with crystalline water. Beatriz brought Estela, who was worried that someone might see us and know that she was with us. Still, she was happy and wanted to go down to the water, an immense natural spring in which we immersed ourselves as in a ritual bathing ceremony. She wore a white shirt that clung to her body and the sensation of immersion in the water was sensual and free. I realized then that through this ritual bath I had recovered my ancient memory and now again I was able to undertake the most extreme and difficult enterprises. Then in a half-dream of waking up, my head was hurting, and it seemed terrible to me that what I had dreamed wasn't true. Talking with Susana, I told her how Lola Hoffman had laughed over this bathing in the 'fountain of youth,' which was how we saw ourselves and how we felt in that water."

"In an early part of the dream I see myself roaming a city in Spain accompanied by Mario Sanchez. The two of us are carrying packages, our hands are full. The town is rather desolate and it seems we're waiting for a bus. When it arrives, I notice that it is packed and that passengers are hanging from the steps. Mario runs and manages to enter through the back door. I, who am also in a frantic hurry, try to get on through the second door. The passengers make way for me and at last I succeed in climbing in, despite the fact that the bus is completely full. The journey continues, we travel through treeless boulevards that remind me of neighborhoods in Quinta Normal in Santiago. At a street crossing the driver asks if any passenger is getting off on the left. No one answers and so the bus begins to climb a slope to our right. I don't see Mario Sanchez but I know that he is in the bus.

Time passes and the same bus is transformed into an underground vehicle. Now it is a subway car in Toronto, rather comfortable, with very few passengers. I see among them a woman who appears sick to the point of death. She tells me that she is the sister of our neighbor Deborah; her face is swollen and it seems she is suffering from a very high fever. I extract from one of my innumerable bags a species of animal bladder in which I carry a medicine: perhaps a water that can cure her. I tell her to lie down on the seat, and I pour water in her mouth, at the same time trying to give her air by waving a kind of fan.

The woman recovers, or more precisely, she is transformed into another of Deborah's sisters. Once more I repeat the program of water-medicine and air, and see that finally she is well and can move and walk. She expresses elaborate thanks; she has had many problems on this trip. I say good-bye and she leaves by a door on the right side: maybe there is one woman, maybe two: it's not clear to me in the dream. I've scarcely returned to my seat when the door on the left opens and now it is Deborah in person who enters, also sick, perhaps with a fever. I tell her that only a few minutes ago I had met her two sisters. I don't know what she answers; she is wearing a type of costume she favored, colored like woven fabric from India. I give her water also and I make her stretch out on the seats—maybe the only way to cure these women.

*That I am the one who cures, like a warlock, does not seem peculiar to
me in the dream.*

*I see myself later in the center of a provincial city. I am walking
with some women friends, or maybe they are only servants. I don't know
really why I have been transformed into a true potentate, supremely
rich. Apparently I am in search of some paintings by my friend Mayo.
A woman with me says we will visit a person who may have important
works by the artist. This woman and a man dressed in black, also ac-
companying me, are quite deformed and their faces appear tubercular,
wrinkled, cracked. We arrive at a mansion on a corner and two women
are waiting for us, one with very short hair who reminds me vaguely of
France, Mayo's wife, and another who is very old and bent. I go up to
the older woman and, kissing her hand, beg pardon for the troubles we
are causing her.*

*The whole place is painted in green tones. First they show me
two small tablets, gold-tinted and vertical, eighty centimeters by forty,
which someone has sent specially so that I could see them. They are
like paintings by the early Renaissance artist, Luca Signorelli. Then I
approach and inspect a very simple piece of furniture that first had been
given a red base coat and then covered with gold laminate on which
were painted figures two or three inches high. The gold has not worn
well and the work reminds me of reproductions of Greek vases. I turn
to examining with care a piece approximately two meters in height sup-
ported on four tiny legs. It is something extraordinary, made with an
imagination and technical proficiency that we have long ago forgotten.
The persons surrounding me try to sell me something else, not grasping
the true spiritual treasure they possess in this work. I look finally at the
left wall of the room where there is a mural approximately three by
seven meters, entirely made with burnished gold leaf, though the fig-
ures and the whole scene depicted are in an intricate relief with special
emphasis and luster. I touch this mural, which pulses with a transcend-
ent throbbing. It is a precious work and only by a true grace could it
have been conceived. It doesn't matter whether I buy it or not, the im-
portant thing is to preserve it, since it constitutes an authentic treasure
of the spirit. I awake full of delight, happy for the rest of the day, feeling
incomparably rich for having seen these images."*

When I visited Mayo some years ago, there was such good rap-
port between us that explanations were unnecessary. His work, of unique
value in our time, is so little known perhaps because of the great in-

wardness of its content. And it had been an example to me to have the privilege of meeting him thus, in his anonymity, a man without pretension, absolutely generous.

"I find myself in an immense room where people are chatting. I realize that I've forgotten an early part of the dream. Seated near me in the place are a woman and two men. One of them is elderly, or seems so due to the salt-and-pepper beard he wears. His clothes are bright. The man tells how he 'fired two shots at the woman, after an argument.' The scene strikes me vividly and it shakes me. I don't know if he means the woman with him or another; seemingly, these events are a matter of indifference to all the rest of the crowd.

A shred of the dream remains with me upon waking. I am in a new house, well arranged in accord with bourgeois taste. Rivka is there and Susana and I, and a small boy who is still in bed. We are going out and I have to use the bathroom. One of the women tells me I should change my shirt; the one I'm wearing is white and I decide to put on a blue one. When I look at myself in the mirror I see not myself but the man who shot at the woman, yet in some way he is myself, for I trim my beard and observe that, with its small cleft, it gives me the look of Mephistopheles. The child, the boy, calls out in the nearby room. I go to the crack open between his door and the wall and look at him: he is lying in a shelf-bed, made of carved wood, which was mine some forty years ago. I feel pressured, because we have to leave."

The Dance–
Images and the Wind

woke up still heavy with sleep, and thought a shower and black coffee might bring me back to the reality I was living. I ran my eye over the room that was so vivid in my memory. In the neighboring one, my sisters were noisily bustling around. I decided to go see what was producing the commotion, and though I never found out for certain, I believe it had to do with the selection of dresses for the dance, an activity to which they assigned the highest importance. Watching from their doorway, I thought it better not to interrupt such a lively gathering. So, since Mother was in the kitchen, I went to talk with her while preparing the coffee I figured would wake me up for the next few hours. My mother, whom I had once seen changed to an old lady stooped with age, was again that precious woman with the fairest of complexions; on her arms and neck delicate blue veins could be seen. She came to me, looked into my eyes and said, My happiness, son, depends in great measure on yours. If in Helena you've found the woman who assumes many faces, I hope that you and she will always be as happy as we are now. I hugged her and said not to worry, that many mysteries had been cleared up for me, and some others I was hoping still to penetrate.

I asked her where my clothes were so that I could choose a suit to wear that evening, but she said that Asmodeus had come by earlier to bring my suit for the dance: I didn't have to worry about it and could dress at leisure in my parents' bedroom; it was still two or three hours before nightfall, so I had time to go find Helena and get ready to receive the evening's guests.

I went out again onto the porch. The desert was changing the colors of the dunes in the magic atmosphere of the last hours before sunset. Far off I saw one of the green cars, a limousine of the thirties, approaching; from it my father and the Maestro emerged, animated as always, talking now in Indonesian, a language I had heard before only from my friend the poet John Schlechter Duvall. They came up to my table, and on my shoulder the marvelous armadillo with teeth of gold began to interpret for me: "They say that they have surprises for you, but their only motive is happiness." Then Leonardo began to speak in Spanish, as if to himself, laughingly commenting that one never knew what dangers came along with having a polyglot translator.

They told me that in the afternoon they had traveled along practically the whole shoreline of the Salar Grande west of the Mountains of Salt and as far south as Llullaillaico. We didn't invite you, they claimed, because you were sleeping so peacefully it would have been criminal to wake you. I smiled: I knew they had been planning something or other for the evening but didn't want to pry after details.

As they talked passionately about the people and life of Borneo and other islands, I saw how much improved in spirits Leonardo seemed. I had always taken for granted that he was at least fifty. Now however he seemed no more than thirty-five. His beard had turned redder and a widebrimmed hat framed his handsome face. Certainly he was a man who had seen much, but it was hard at this moment to acknowledge the reality that his life extended through millennia. Suddenly he spoke: Dear Ludwig, if it seems to you there are changes in me, it's because the image of your inner demon has changed. You've arrived at an equilibrium in which I am a man with your own characteristics.

He laughed at my surprised expression and went on: Within an hour night will fall, you and Helena will welcome your guests; if you need me for anything I'll be there, talking with old friends. Now let's make our preparations.

I went to the bedroom to dress and was startled by the lapis lazuli color of my suit, accompanied by shoes and accessories in a rock gray. Asmodeus put his head in and told me that in the dances the Maestro held all the gentlemen wore severe black and the ladies transparent dresses, but since this event was according to my desires, he had used every variety of costume and ornament. He brought me, as well, a walking stick with an ivory head exactly fitted to my hand. When I finished dressing I went out on the porch and found the green car standing ready.

I got in and without a word being said the machine took me to the guest hostel where Helena was waiting for me. I rang the bell with curiosity; what color would her dress be? She appeared wrapped in a violet cape that covered her completely, her high collar forming a beautiful halo of pearls and filigree around her face. Her embrace and her lips made me forget whatever worry I still felt about the dance. Night had come and several hours would pass before the moon rose. Let's go, she laughed, we mustn't let the guests find no one there to welcome them.

The automobile carried us quickly beyond Río Loa and away from accustomed roads, traveling toward the San Pedro volcano to take us out to the Desert of Salt. As we moved onto the flats of that ancient plain of water, it surprised me to see intense floodlights illuminating an enormous hand of stone, its palm turned upward. The sculpture was twenty or twenty-five meters high: as I told Helena, I had never seen it there. Laughing, hugging me, she said it was there to show the way to those who had not visited in the region before. I noticed then that, leading from the monumental hand, immense torches had been set up. They produced a show of light visible from very far away, and it was easy, guided by them, to find the place designated for the dance. What we first saw of it, from far off, was several immense shops and stores built of a material that reminded me of mother-of-pearl or some similar marine substance, the ensemble of strange structures seeming at once bizarre and attractive, as does every unknown thing. The car stopped and I could see that exuberant vegetation had till now blocked from sight the large number of fountains and statues surrounding the central building.

I gave my arm to Helena and we ascended a stair above which the great entranceway of the place was set, very high up, about sixty or seventy meters. It was entirely screened by a huge metal cutout which, after having remained in place for some moments, disappeared as though it had been only an effect of the flames that lit up the immense antechamber beyond. Crews of servants, their dark oiled skin contrasting with gold adornments, were carrying things at a run from one spot to another. Their chief, or at any rate the man directing them, approached us and making a profound obeisance indicated that the adjoining hall was the ballroom. But it was hard to leave such an exotic setting and the fine view we had. Clearly, everyone arriving would have to pass through this entrance hall, so we decided to wait there; in the distance we could already see caravans of cars advancing over the bleached plains of salt.

First to arrive were the Maestro and my parents, followed by Zoila Campana, on the arm of someone I couldn't believe I was seeing, Rolando Toro, my old and beloved friend, the inventor of "biodance" among so many other things. We embraced, almost in tears, filled with powerful feelings. Leonardo came up and said in apologetic tones: I've allowed myself to take him from his usual duties for this evening, and in order to make you feel easier I'd like to confer on him the title of Grand Master of Dances. We applauded this and Leonardo handed Rolando a baton finely worked in gold so that my friend could direct the dancers and musicians. The crystal bell rang to announce the arrival of each new couple. Many of the villagers I could scarcely recall; others were so present in my memory that I recognized them from far off. Each one embraced me and kissed Helena's hand. Juan Siglic came with his wife, extraordinarily beautiful in a dress of tulle; José Kruger, gallant as always, was on Katty's arm and behind them Kuni with Pedro Garzón, then Ida, escorted by a very dear friend, Hernán Baeza, carrying his guitar.

Next my brother Carlos approached, laughing, accompanied by a woman wrapped in veils like those worn in northern Africa. He embraced me and said: You've always wanted to put certain questions to the Queen of Sheba—here she is, in front of you, in person. I saw her turn her brown face and smile at my confusion; placing her hand on my chest, she said, This is your best counselor, kissed Helena, and went arm in arm with my brother to the dance floor.

Alone and as if talking to himself, my friend Martín Cerda arrived and, embracing me, whispered in my ear: Guess what? Father Gregorio read your poem about him and told me to deliver an answer. As in schooldays, we laughed together, and he disappeared into the depths of the room where young men and beautiful girls were serving liquor. Then we greeted Doctor Sarabia and his wife, who seemed more worried about the rhythms of the dance than anything else. Next came the Rossos—he slender in his dark suit and Assunta, his wife, immense as a globe—followed by Gustavo Schutt and Sara, in an African costume that fit her like her true skin.

I heard the bell clamor loudly: here was my friend Viterbo Sepúlveda, smiling on the arm of Salome, the stepdaughter of the Tetrarch of Galilee. With a broad grin, Viterbo explained: They let me choose and I chose her, since at the end of the evening, without any danger to John, she can dance for us the dance of the seven veils. He hadn't chosen badly: seeing Viterbo and Salome together, one could understand Herod's madness.

Again and again the bell sounded and I was greeted and embraced by a veritable multitude of people, among whom I noticed three who weren't from Río Loa. When they were closer, emotion made my heart leap: there were Franz Schubert and Robert Schumann with his adored Clara. I felt that many of my desires had been fulfilled this night and little remained to wish for; unimaginably, I could embrace the musicians who so often had consoled me with their pains. Wrapped up in their joy, they saluted us, kissing Helena, and proceeded to the ballroom where they were received with general applause.

I turned and hugged Helena, who shone like a statue of soft ivory, her charms encircled with strands of pearls. She folded me in her arms and whispered in my ear: Ludwig, we still haven't finished.

Two last cars were arriving and I heard the ringing of the crystal bell. A man I didn't recognize got out of the first car: not very tall and with a certain informality in his dress. Gallantly he offered his hand to a lovely young woman dressed in the ancient Egyptian style. Suddenly I realized that it was Oscar de Lubicz Milosz and the marvelous Queen Karomama. There was silence when they entered; greeting me affectionately, he said: Your desires have permitted me to complete my own. Karomama was radiant in an iridescent dress covered with the feathers of her guardian deities; how soft she seemed beneath her plaited hair, arranged like a helmet in the manner of the Libyan nobility to which her family belonged. She looked deeply into my eyes and said: Your desires are strange, because they produce happiness. I've brought these lilies that grow in the gardens near the Delta for your beautiful companion. They hugged each other and I knew I could never forget that image.

I noticed another car stopping at the door, so I asked them to go in to the dance.

A gentleman dressed in black came up the steps, followed by a beautiful woman whose hair floated on the wind. I had never before seen him except in poor engravings and I bowed in respect: Don Luis de Góngora y Argote, welcome! He responded: I am the one who should thank you. He presented the woman with him and I saw that she had a long branch of red roses fastened to her breast, which caused drops of blood to fall like petals as she walked. No verse is free, Don Luis said. Or maybe this is my chance to see if the poet can be redeemed, even once, from what he has written.

I invited them to go in, and since we saw no other cars in the distance, we all followed Helena to the ballroom. From the entrance we observed how Rolando had arranged the dancing: the orchestra was invisible and toward the back there were groups of guests making toasts and conversation. We decided to dance to the other side of the room: Helena transformed me into a feather that fluttered to the beat of the music. This play of wholly novel caresses absorbed us and brought us to where we could see Karomama with a ritual step teaching Milosz to dance in the ancient manner of the Egyptians. Schumann let Clara's head rest on his chest: one could tell they were moving to their own melody. Don Luis too was dancing, but his look was troubled. When we reached the other side, where the talk was keeping many of the guests laughing happily, I went over to Leonardo and whispered: Why can't such an extraordinary poet as Góngora find happiness in this party? I'm bad at remembering verses, he told me. Maybe you can remember that tercet where he asks those who come after him to pause an instant and consider the footprints that, in the earth...

"we leave behind us, mine in blood, yours in flowers,"

I quoted, as if hearing an old song.

Let's see about contenting Don Luis, the Maestro responded. Each drop of blood will become a flower and the carnivorous roses on the breast of the unknown woman will turn white. And indeed, before long we saw the old prelate frisking to chords dictated by my beloved Rolando's baton.

The music at times turned sweet and caressing, at other times sharp, like ice before it breaks up. Rolando Toro seemed in truth born for this job of Grand Master of Dances. At the far extreme of the room Schubert was playing newly composed pieces for some aficionados. His small eyeglasses seemed to illuminate his round, sensual face. Ida asked him how certain of his compositions had come to be written, and Hernán Baeza sang him songs of the Altiplano, accompanying himself on the guitar. Palpably, they all were enjoying something that they had dreamed of at some point in their lives: encounters with beloved beings, lost years suddenly recovered, perfumes and garments assembled from all parts of the planet.

While I held Helena in a kind of dream, the crystal bell rang and the Dance Master asked for a few minutes—or maybe hours—of attention. Now, he said, the beautiful Salome is going to perform the dance of the seven veils, something people have talked about for centuries.

But no one has had the opportunity, like you, to see her in person. Now, thanks to the choice of the artist Viterbo Sepúlveda, you can all enjoy yourselves, and without fear, since no one is going to cut off anyone's head.

A column of dense smoke began to move over a platform that floated about two feet above the floor, and a captivating scent accompanied this movement of smoke and of veils of tulle in the most diverse colors. Through the languid smoke we saw long strips of scarlet muslin surging and pausing in the air, followed by repeated gestures that seemed to want to disclose, as with a hook, some infinitely delicate creature. When the covering of smoke and the large multicolored bands had been removed, we saw Salome dancing almost motionlessly. Her body seemed naked but had always a new secret to reveal to the eye, and if at times the wind covered her and we believed she was on the point of disappearing, it was only so that, denuding herself even from all skin, she could permit us to dream things never imagined. At the sixth veil she made a grimace of sorrow and began to dance on her hands, leaving her body to our imagination—her body, which exploded before our eyes like an ocean. It was an eternal rebirth in which each of us lost the sense of time; it was the tide of desire that never ends.

The smoke enwrapped her, and now in tongues of fire we had to hope that our sensibility could breathe at last, to assure us that her image was dancing inside us.

When the sound of the oboes died out and the performance had been blown away by the desert breeze, we knew once and for all that this dance and no other marvel had maddened the Tetrarch of Galilee.

Applause broke over the room like waves, and I had the sense that sometimes the marvelous so overwhelms us that we can't resist it. Don Luis came up and, making a bow to the Maestro, recited with a light in his eyes:

"They will leave you little, these hours—
The hours that are wearing away the days,
The days that are blotting out the years."

And yet, he said, and I saw him smile, it is sometimes permitted that even poets can be redeemed by the power of love. The woman with him gave her branch of roses—now white—to Helena and we saw that if any trace of her presence lingered in them, it took the form of the petals and their delicate fragrance. The time had grown very late, and the moon that had shone throughout the dance began to decline toward the west, hanging close above the Green Lemon Hills. One group after another came to say good-bye, exchange a few words, or simply embrace us. I saw Milosz looking at us as though from his dream of an eternal childhood, while my good friend Martín explained to me one more time that he had seen Father Gregorio, who had suggested a response to my poem, but the strength of his emotion had made him forget it.

Little by little, in that immense mother-of-pearl-like shell, the wind began to blow, and we saw that the last guests had gone away. I took Helena in my arms and I led her to the waiting green car. What else could I ask for? Ahead of us, Leonardo was walking with my parents and I dropped into the limousine's back seat and into a long dream. The party I had planned so many times was over; now I could do nothing more than suppose it would never be possible again. The slopes of the high mountains brightened and came into view more clearly; it was time to return.

The Return

awoke very late; noon had already passed.

Helena was singing beside me, a melody like a recollection of many vivid things that revolve again and again in memory. She gave me a lingering kiss and said, Ludwig dear, every day when you wake, every moment that you think about me, I'm at your side. The images of our loved ones trouble us terribly, but it's essential to understand that we carry them inside us, we're united to them forever.

I dressed quickly when Helena told me they were waiting for us at my parents' house for a small lunch. Apparently, various important things had to be decided. In the distance, Río Loa presented the aspect of all oases, quiet beneath its trees. My emotions had been so strong that now I felt each breeze or wind changed the landscape and its inhabitants, those beings so yearned for and now present to me.

The gathering at our house was sparkling and joyful. With the help of Asmodeus, Mother had arranged things so that the guests, and there were a lot of them, were at ease and could enjoy the pleasures of friendship. Seemingly everyone who had attended the dance was here now to thank me for the invitation and to greet the Maestro. How was it that so many people could fit in such a small village? I didn't know, although I had seen the wonders that Leonardo had accomplished in recent days. Next to him sat Schubert and Schumann, accompanied by Milosz and the superb Karomama. When the Maestro saw me, he motioned me over. After greeting everyone, I joined Leonardo, who gently told me that as the moon was waning, he had to leave. You've given me

137

such joy, inviting me to your village, he said. At every moment, friendship has made me feel a part of it. I saw that he was happy, with no vestige of the melancholy proverbial with him.

Here you are, with all the friends of your youth, and I'd like to drink a toast to their happiness. They raised their cups and I saw Don Luis laugh. He was chatting with Milosz and recalling old verses. Viterbo, Rolando (who never abandoned the delightful Salome for an instant), my brother and sisters, all raising their cups, wished that my old desires might be fulfilled forever. Their images passed one by one before me, sweet, conserved so clearly in my memory. It might seem that time had stopped yet I knew beyond doubt, by the changes of the music and the reflection of light in the trees, that now the beloved verses by Sidney Keyes were true:

"And those in the garden will understand
That time is a thief who does not relent..."

Helena took me by the arm and, drawing me to her heart, said: It shouldn't be that a few verses make you sad. I agreed, laughing over the clairvoyance of what she said. Leonardo stood and grasped my shoulders: You've given all of us great happiness—even me, hardened by many battles. But I have to invite everyone to cross to the other side of the river where a balloon is being inflated, with space for all who want to come with me. At the end of the afternoon the wind will be cold and we can begin the voyage without any problem. As to you, dear poet, I believe you now know with certainty that love is eternal. Though I can't always be visible, I leave you our beloved Helena Ferrucchi—she'll guide you on the ways you still don't understand or haven't yet been called to follow.

I watched the passing of that festive lunch—now it had already been over for hours, and I couldn't avoid feeling the gnawing worm of melancholy. Schubert, in contrast, intoned a joyful song and I saw that in groups and pairs all the multitude was moving toward the river. My mother, on Father's arm, asked Helena and me to come with her. It was a sweet promenade full of dreams and joys. Sara was still gleaming in her dancing costume and accompanied her own movements with songs her grandmother had taught her. Kruger laughed with my sisters and Martín chatted away, dazzled by his encounter with Góngora.

Upon arriving at the river, we saw the top part of an immense balloon across the mudflats. The gas envelope was almost as large as the village itself; cables secured the spacious gondola where the passengers would ride. Leonardo took me by the arm and assured me that he would drop off each person in his or her particular world. I think that for you, on the other hand, he said, it would be better to remain tonight in the village. Tomorrow you'll see other things that you don't yet know, and the train will be waiting for you at the station. It was hard to say good-bye to this friend, a friend whom through ignorance I had so feared. Embracing me, he whispered: We'll see each other in the future.

I stopped at the foot of the gangplank and was moved to embrace each one who went up, with a deep, inevitable emotion. Among the many beloved beings going aboard, I saw Gaspar, Judith and Salome mounted on their giant ostriches; they were making funny faces at me as though to say, we'll be back. They resembled an old engraving of the exotic specimens walking into the Ark. Now only fifteen or twenty persons remained, villagers whom I scarcely recognized. My parents, my brother and sisters, my beloved friends were waving to me. Often we fell silent and tears clouded our eyes. The last to embark was Leonardo, who grasped me to him and repeated that we'd see each other soon.

The pilots untied the moorings and the immense, majestic balloon rose slowly against a darkening indigo sky; with it were vanishing entire fragments of my life, of the dimensions of being, of landscapes that continually changed color. Minutes passed and as darkness deepened, we watched the airship rising over the hills of the desert, illuminated as though from inside, until it was only one more point among the stars, impossible to distinguish from the other minuscule lights.

Helena took my arm, chanting a song that told me it was time to go back. The others who had remained on earth, a little like shadows, went with us, inhabitants of the village I did not remember because they had lived in it in another time. We arrived at my parents' house and decided to pass the night there; the darkness was not complete and as the wind began to howl over the old, beloved pepper trees, Helena brought a platter with fruits and sweets.

I want you to understand with total confidence, she said, that I'm at your side always, because it's in your love that my true destiny lies. If at times you believe you are alone, it's due to a distortion of time; you possess me and all my faces in the book with ivory covers. I am not as many women as you sometimes believe—there is one image, which repeats itself, searching for the threads of likeness.

I felt that past emotion had left me exhausted. I laid my head on the heart of the one woman who meant everything to me, and dream returned and broke once more against the rocks of reality, that other dream, infinite in its variations, which also can be mysterious and bewitching.

I awoke with an intense headache.

I heard noises in the next room, and when I opened my eyes I noticed that the bedroom had gotten smaller and was painted and furnished in a strange manner. Near my bed I saw the suitcases I had prepared for the trip. However, these images seemed so pallid that I ran to the bathroom for a shower; after that I had to accept that maybe I was awake, but what I saw had nothing to do with what I had lived through in recent days. On my way to the dining room I met a rather timid man of about thirty. He greeted me kindly, but he was also rather afraid. Who are you? I asked. And where are my parents?

Sir, the stranger responded feebly, my name is Efraín Hernández and I'm one of the teachers in this little village. As it happens, in recent days the whole village has suffered incredible enchantments and we've seen absolutely unknown people walking among us and not seeming to see us. You're one of the few that haven't disappeared like an effect of the wind. A lot of the villagers thought it was a general spell. Work at the factory stopped for days, since it's dangerous to have strangers moving among us; the children were taken over to Calama—their fear of the strangers' presence was making them cry. He clearly wanted to rid himself of a heavy weight; giving me not a second to question him, he went on to say that some workers who knew the village since childhood had told him it was a mystery, the strangers seemingly were people who had lived here some sixty years ago. The desire to keep talking overpowered him, and he had the open-heartedness characteristic of school teachers.

I asked him if he'd give me a little cup of coffee, which sent him running to the kitchen to bring a tray with what I had requested plus some sweet rolls. The noises I'd been hearing had ceased; they had come from two children terrified that their father was chatting with a ghost; now they chose to peer at me through a crack in the door.

And the teacher Zoila Campana, do you know her? I asked him. I've only seen her in an old photograph in the school, he replied. She was engaged here many years ago—we think she was the first teacher who ever came to live in this village.

I could scarcely contain myself. I got up from the table and went to the window that looked out on the garden beyond which the delicate

Zoila had lived. But everything was different now. The garden between the two houses had disappeared. Only a few dry stalks gave testimony to the greenery that had once existed.

The teacher invited me to go out and tour the village. I see that you are not a ghost, he said, conquering his fear. We went outside. How transformed the porch was, and how dusty everything seemed. In the last few days, my companion told me, we all must have been victims of some sorcery. We saw houses and heard beings we had never known before.

And you, have you ever lived here? he asked me carefully.

Many years ago, I said, in that house where you live now. Once it was very different; I was born in this village, and don't be frightened. I'm not a dead man come from the grave. I've made a trip here with some friends who wanted to see Río Loa, that's all.

He seemed to breathe more easily. But the immense balloon on which your friends left, is it going to return? I don't know, I said. As I walked around, I saw that whole rows of houses were gone, with only remains of rock and cement recalling their former locations. We passed through the square, which was almost abandoned and without its benches. There the pepper trees had resisted the drought, but how melancholy it was to see the old general store, and ruins of buildings that recalled whole families for me: the Sienas, the Quirogas, Labarca, Gaona and many others. The teacher seemed to sense the emotion that had overcome me and walked in silence three or four meters back. Recalling Don Luis, I murmured:

> "...but you and they together
> in the earth, in smoke, in dust, in shadow, in
>   nothingness."

What are you saying? the teacher asked me. Nothing, nothing. Some verses that come to mind, in memory of an extraordinary friend. We walked all around the village, and as we returned to the house that was now the schoolmaster's, the stir of a light breeze was like a blessing to me.

Is there anyone who can help me carry my suitcase? I asked. Seemingly the rest of the inhabitants were hiding or had run away for a few days to other towns. He told me that he would take me to the station, supposing that I meant to make the trip on foot, since those ancient dark limousines seemed only to have been part of a fantastic nightmare.

He hefted my suitcase on his shoulder, so I was able to keep turning back to look at the nondescript little village from far away. We passed a house where Ida had lived when grown and I saw that is was all closed up, the curtains drawn—out of fear, no doubt, that I might see someone. In front of the entrance to the dynamite factory there was a military unit quartered. They're as perplexed as the rest of the villagers, the teacher told me. They don't know what to do about those darkened pullman cars standing in the station with no one in them.

I saw the cars up ahead. Then I was at the railway station itself, but I did not find Don Ricardo Lorca, nor the gardens of which he was so proud. What had become of them? Had they been only a mirage?

The schoolmaster had carried my suitcase more than two kilometers and now grew bold enough to ask me, Do you know what's been happening here? I laughed and told him, It's a question of destiny. Many years ago a poet was born here whose great passion was for dreaming. And since dreams are another, parallel life, someone very powerful allowed him to return to this village where, between dust and wind, his dreams were nurtured. He looked at me wide-eyed. Yes, I said to him, there are things that are possible to live only in dreams.

A little fearfully, he put my suitcase into one of the train cars, to which he seemed to attribute a life of their own. They were indeed empty and next to the old platform I read the lettering: Río Loa. I stood there a few more minutes with that open-hearted teacher, Efraín Hernández. Maybe, I told him, without your knowing it, you yourself have a poet among your children. I offered him my hand and assured him again he had nothing to fear. Within a few minutes I would be on my way back to the far north, that point the witches always seek. I got into the center car, the one in which I had arrived, and waved good-bye to him through the windows.

Off in the distance I could see the snow-capped peaks of the volcanoes—How strange, I thought, how different, how close surrealism is to those of us born on this continent. I heard a bell sound and the three dark cars that had caused such fear in the local people moved out of the station.

Now I sat alone in the spacious passenger coach and a pang of nostalgia made me realize that in a way a precious adventure was ending; that at first I had been afraid of and later had adored Helena; that I had glimpsed the face of Leonardo and then the days had converted his terrible features into those of a beloved friend. In this return to the far north I felt the sensation of loneliness.

Then from the front of the car I saw a friendly, smiling young man coming toward me. Our orders are to make you happy. If you want anything, call us and we'll bring it at once. I thanked him with a gesture. What could I want? Hadn't my dreams been fulfilled?

Anyway, the young man announced to me in a friendly way, you can go to another car, maybe it will be more comfortable for resting. I followed his advice. The windows in the next car were longer and the countryside passed quickly.

I would have liked to ask Helena something, to be able to put my head in her lap. Then I remembered the small book with painted ivory covers. I looked at it a long time before opening it: how beautiful it was! Then I lifted the cover at random and a beautiful pheasant leapt out onto my table. Its face was Helena's. Laughing, it said to me: Beloved, you've had too much excitement, you have to rest now. I'm with you, my feathers will cover you in your dream.

I caressed her face, and I saw that the small armadillo was talking with Helena. When he awakes, she told him, we will be very near Toronto, the place of meetings.

It seemed to me that I could feel again the beating of love in the wings of the bird, and then I was submerged in dream. How much time passed? What distances ran down those always parallel rails? I will never know.

On waking, I saw the shoreline of a blue lake crossed by a multitude of sails. On my shoulder the armadillo was gazing at the crystal water. Within a few moments we would be in Toronto.

Now the train cars were slowly entering the station.

On the platform I saw Susana waving to me with a bouquet of lilies.

Returning to her was coming back anew to another reality. You don't have to run, the young man said. I'll take your suitcase to the car. Then Susana was there, laughing and embracing me. What have you forgotten this time? she asked, and I could assure her that nothing was lost: I had never had to open the suitcase. Would she somehow be able to understand?

I've got two treasures, I told her. You'll see them later. They're secrets hidden in the desert that cannot stay silent when the whirlwind is moving over the sand.

AGMV
MARQUIS
Québec, Canada
1999